CW00469336

The Baging

© N.C. Lewis 2019

Reader's Note

THIS BOOK IS SET IN the small coastal town of Cromer in the county of Norfolk, England and makes use of British English (although one or two American words or spellings might have slipped past me).

Cromer is an ancient town, a modern community and a hidden gem of a seaside resort. I hope one day you will get to visit. When you do, please write and let me know how it went. You can reach me at: info@nclewis.com

Chapter 1

SUNDAY, MARCH 25, 1923

The late afternoon sunlight sparkled and shimmered across the deep greens and browns of the Norfolk countryside. Across the entire landscape, pink and white blossoms bloomed on the trees. Sheep grazed lazily on the slopes, and the cries of flocks of blackbirds sounded in harmony with the rhythmic rattle of the steam train as it clattered towards the town of Cromer.

I had the entire compartment to myself, rested my leatherbound journal in my lap and idly watched the hedgerows, farms, and hamlets roll by. It was seventeen years since I moved away with my father and sister. I was a fresh-faced, twenty-five-year-old girl from the country then. Now I'm forty-two, weary, and unmarried.

As I watched the rural scenery flit by, memories of a half-forgotten life flooded back. I remembered our little russet-bricked cottage with the slanted tile roof that sat perched at the end of a narrow lane and the dirt path that led to the cliff with the steep, jagged steps down to the rocky beach. There was old Mr Gunthorpe with his short trousers and wooden clogs, the Victorian schoolhouse, the ancient, grey-stoned Saint Magdalene church, and the King's Head Tavern where Father drank away his Sunday afternoons.

And I remembered Mother. "Maggie, you give up on things too easily. Whatever you start, see it through. Be persistent but polite."

Seventeen years since she died.

Seventeen years since my sister, Nancy's, birth.

The train slowed to a crawl as the track curved around a sharp bend. Iron wheels screeched; the steam whistle tooted; the carriages rocked and shuddered.

Within three months of Mother passing, we moved to London. Father said business in the capital city was booming, and to believe the newspaper reports, nuggets of gold paved the streets. But I suspect it was to get away from Cromer and the memories of what happened to Mother.

In London, Father sunk what little money we had into a fish shop on Seven Sisters Road.

The shop did not prosper.

Father turned his hand to stone masonry, and when that did not work out, went into the horse-drawn cab trade. But the business collapsed as motor vehicles replaced horses, and Father was once again unemployed, this time for nearly three months. That's when he bought Nancy a mangle so she could earn a little money by taking in laundry.

Soon after, Father gave up self-employment for work in a bakery shop and took to smoking a clay pipe in the evenings. One night as he read the newspaper by lamplight, he said, "Maggie, you'll be fine when I'm long gone. It is little Nancy that grieves my heart. What will she do when my time is up?"

Nancy suffers from terrible spasms in the warmer months and bone-shaking coughs when the cold sets in. Undersized for her age, she was born unable to hear and cannot speak.

"When I am gone, you will care for Nancy. Promise me that, Maggie."

Quietly, I had resolved I would do exactly as my father had asked. That was one promise I wouldn't break. And now as Father grows old and Nancy's health worsens, I wondered whether I was doing the right thing leaving them alone in London.

The train whistle sounded three shrill blasts. I looked through the window. A herd of cattle clambered through a gap in the hedgerow. A scrawny man, with a cloth hat and large pole, yelled and steered the tan-and-white animals away from the railway track. Two young boys, dressed almost in rags, ran alongside the herd—a family of farmworkers. And to look at them, more unfortunate than the street urchins that populated the cobbled streets of London.

The boys waved. I opened the carriage window, waved back, then settled deep into my seat. The train picked up speed.

I'm moving back to Cromer to work as a bookkeeper for my uncle, Tristan Harbottle—my mother's younger brother. Uncle Tristan had tried his hand at many things—a poet, abstract sculptor, photography portrait artist, novelist. He had even worked in a travelling circus and lived in America. Tristan's Hands, a staffing agency, was his latest venture. It supplied workers to wealthy families: maids, butlers, cooks, and gardeners.

Father was unhappy with the move. "Why go back to Norfolk, Maggie? Why are you leaving the capital city to go back to a rural backwater?"

I'd tried to explain about Uncle Tristan and his business, about my memories of Mother, and the need to return to my roots.

"Well," Father had said, "Uncle Tristan has matured over the years and put his boyish pastimes and tomfoolery behind him. He has written to me of his latest business ventures, which I feel will be very profitable. Whatever you learn about running a successful business, write and tell me. I've not given up hope of one day being my own boss again, so I can earn enough to help provide for Nancy when I'm gone."

I unfolded Uncle Tristan's letter and read the thin, untidy handwriting.

Dear Maggie,

Oh yes. Yes, and once again, yes! Leave the grimy confines of London. Come home to the fresh air and infinite freedom of the Norfolk coast. Here on the seashore, the living is easy, inexpensive, and relaxed, and you will make an excellent clerk for Tristan's Hands. Lord knows I need one. The enterprise has become somewhat of a strain on my artistic pursuits. A burden made doubly troublesome by a lack of a wife and children to help. I'm afraid I just don't have the business nose of your father.

You write of your "utter" lack of bookkeeping knowledge. Well, I never could figure it out myself. The artist's mind isn't wired that way. But I am as certain as Christmas, you will pick it up. And you shall start with the Sandoe account—Sir Richard Sandoe and his charming aunt, Lady Louisa Herriman. All will be explained when we meet.

I gazed at the countryside. The train was clattering along a narrow valley which opened into a hamlet with tiny, russet-brick houses. I had never heard of Sir Sandoe before, but the name raised a picture of a tall, elegant gentleman with the charm and grace of royalty.

And Lady Herriman, what was she like? All pearls, silk gowns, and elegance. Yes, they were beginning to take shape. It all sounded so glamorous. Quite different from my previous position—shop assistant for the stout, short-tempered Mr Pritchard in his pie-and-mash shop on Darlington Road. There I'd served jellied eels, meat pies, and mashed potatoes to a hoard of eager Londoners.

On my first day behind the counter, Mr Pritchard had said, "I shall pay you above the going rate, and soon you will have the money to build a better future." It was a wonderful job until he demanded I become his sweetheart. He is married with seven children.

I turned back to the letter and read on.

Now, I have arranged accommodation for you at Mrs Rusbridger's excellent dwellings. A tranquil boarding house where you can look forward to quiet, peaceful, lamplit evenings to practise your calligraphic penmanship. The kindly lodgings offer a room with a comfortable bed, a hearty breakfast as well as a delicious evening meal. Oh what a time you will have!

We shall celebrate your arrival with a feast. Only the best Norfolk offers for my wonderful niece!

How is your father getting along? I know his ailments are a profound source of worry for you (and me too). I hear he is in the bread-baking business. Londoners love their daily, fresh baked bread; he must be making a good living. I have written to him about my latest business ventures, and they meet with his approval.

Let us agree to discuss financial matters on your arrival. For now, I enclose a first-class train ticket and look forward to hearing about all the new business ideas you have gained in London.

I shall be at Cromer train station to meet you.

Warmly Yours,

Uncle Tristan.

P.S. Give Nancy a warm hug and lots of kisses from her old uncle.

P.P.S. I am sure your father will grow to appreciate the wisdom of your move, even if the memories of what happened to your mother are too painful for him to contemplate a return to the bosom of his ancestors.

Once I'd settled, I'd send for Nancy and pray Father would follow. With only five shillings in my purse, that day was some way off. I needed to earn a little more of the king's currency. But I had a vision, a plan, and determination to get to my destination.

Time would soon tell whether I'd make a success of things.

Chapter 2

THE TRAIN SLOWED AS it pulled into the city of Norwich, shuddering to a stop at an extended wooden platform: carriage doors opened; steam hissed from the idle engine. The platform filled then emptied of people.

I placed Uncle Tristan's letter in my bag, took out a pencil, and practised calligraphic penmanship. I'd taken up calligraphy as a pastime in London. For several minutes, I sketched Gaelic characters. The acute accents over the vowels offered a particular challenge.

The door to my carriage opened.

A stranger entered, stood plumb in the middle of the compartment, feet apart, hands on hips, looking like a Shakespearean actor on the London stage. He was a short little man respectably dressed in a tweed jacket with matching trousers, a white shirt with heavy-starched collars, and a brown fedora hat.

I suppose he was in his late fifties with the leathery countenance of a hunting man. He had peculiarly arched nostrils and his elongated face, like that of a barnyard donkey, served only to emphasise his weathered skin and wide, dark eyes. They were owl-like and seemed to take in everything all at once: my pencil, my journal, my dress, coat, cloche hat, and even my small trunk, which the train guard had placed so carefully on an overhead rack.

"Good afternoon," said the short little man as he raised his fedora. There was a richness to his voice, a superior, plummy accent typical to the English upper class. But he slurred his words, and his breath oozed with brandy or whisky or both. "This seat is vacant, I take it?"

Oh bother!

I clutched my pencil tight in my right hand, annoyed at allowing such an unladylike expression to enter my mind. I'd enjoyed the solitude of the carriage and didn't want to share the space. With a guilty flush, I said, "Indeed it is. It seems we are in luck and have the carriage to ourselves."

"Excellent!" He took the seat directly opposite, unfolded a battered copy of the *Norfolk News,* held it high in front of his face with his arms extended like the captain of a ship might grasp a telescope. "Ah-ha," he said as if to himself, "my stocks are doing rather well."

For a moment, I watched, then relieved he wasn't about to make further conversation, let my eyes drift back to my journal. There were only two stops left on my journey—Bagington Hall then Cromer. With a renewed determination, I continued my penmanship practice. So complete was my concentration that the sound of the steam whistle and low groan of wood and metal, as the train pulled out of Norwich station, barely touched my conscious mind.

As the train picked up speed, I knew I was being observed. In London, watching and being watched is a natural everyday occurrence. You notice the milkman who delivers at such-and-such an hour, and your neighbour calls if they don't see you return from work at your regular time. There is a certain comfort in that, a natural ebb and flow. But here in the tiny confines of a rickety steam train carriage, with a strange man, it was a most unwelcome and somewhat unnerving experience.

I stole a glance at the man. He continued to hold the newspaper high in front of his face.

Don't be silly, Maggie, I told myself. The gentleman is reading, and there is no one else in the carriage.

With a slow movement of my head, I turned from the man and looked through the window. The sun glowed from behind the tree-line streaking the countryside with varying hues of red, orange, and gold. Cattle chewed their cud in the shade of a copse of ancient oak trees, and a scruffy, brown dog galloped alongside the railway track as if trying to outrun the train.

I wrenched my mind back to the journal, picked up the pencil, and concentrated on the acute accents over the Gaelic vowels. As I was finishing a delicate swirl, I suddenly had the feeling, once again, that I was being watched. I turned towards the carriage hallway expecting to see the ticket collector peering through the glass window of the door.

There was no one at the entrance, only the darkened hallway beyond.

Now I felt slightly foolish. Who would be watching?

With determination, I continued my penmanship practice. But the haphazard rock of the carriage as the train slowed to climb a steep incline threw off my hand. Untidy, black scribbles dotted the paper. I put down my journal and pencil then stole another glance at the man.

Through two circular slits cut into the newspaper, a pair of dark eyes stared back.

Chapter 3

"SIR, DO YOU MAKE A regular practice of watching women through peepholes in your newspaper?" My voice was calm and firm, although inside, my stomach flipped like a pancake in a frying pan.

The *Norfolk News* trembled then slowly lowered. With great care, the man folded it. After gazing at me for a few moments, he peeled back his lips into a doglike smirk. "Suffragette."

The word hung in the air as if it explained everything.

I glanced warily at the man. "Pardon?"

"Damn suffragettes have the whole country in an uproar."

Jolly good thing, had trembled on my lips but never passed them. I didn't want to make a scene. "Really?"

"Thought you might be one of the buggers." Again came the doggish smile. "A woman travelling alone, don't you know."

In London, I travelled on the underground trains, overground railways, and omnibuses by myself. But I knew in the rural countryside, everyone knew everyone's business and felt it part of their business to comment on it. And a woman travelling unaccompanied in first class was something to be noted and gossiped about.

I said, "There is nothing in the least bit unusual about my travel arrangements."

The man leaned forward and lowered his voice as if to impart a secret. "I visited Finland a few years back; the place is swarming with women members of parliament. The first country to allow that." He adjusted his fedora. "The Finnish nation has gone to the dogs!"

Riled by the man's impudence, I took a deep breath to calm the fury that brewed in my stomach. "Sir," I began in an even tone, "I take it you are not in favour of the universal franchise?"

"Good God, woman, no!"

l said, "Do you have a daughter?"

There was an almost imperceptible hesitation. "Oh yes, Antoinette was a lovely little thing, quite regal, don't you know. Read Latin, French, Gaelic, and German. Even taught the chambermaid and head butler to read the languages. Quite a character, really." Something seemed to catch in his throat. After a moment, he continued, "Then she got to reading and thinking about politics. The silly girl even petitioned for women to join the Norfolk Workers Agricultural Union."

Enlightened offspring, I thought and wanted to let him know his daughter's outlook bode well for the future of the country. But not wanting an argument, I said, "Where is Antoinette now?"

His eyes turned cold and hard. "Sharrington Insane Asylum."

I sat in shock as his words sunk in. "Dear God! You put your own daughter away?"

"It's been three years."

"How could you?" I made up my mind that I would visit the poor girl as soon as I settled into Cromer. I've never visited Sharrington, but it was local, and now I had a very good reason. "What is your full name, sir?"

The man turned his gaze to the window. "Do you hunt?"

He was clearly too impolite to answer my question. It didn't matter; I knew his daughter's name, Antoinette, and that was enough.

I said, "I find no sport in killing innocent creatures."

"Enjoy a good roast?"

I'd had enough of the terrible little man and said, "I really ought to get back to my penmanship. I hope you don't mind."

"Cabbage, roast beef with lashings of gravy, eh?"

"Have you tried your hand at calligraphy?"

"I like to shoot game and finish them with a knife."

I turned towards the carriage hallway. Where was the ticket inspector?

I said, "Goodness!"

"The hunt, the chase, the kill." His owl-like eyes became very large.

"I see."

"I fought in the Great War, you know."

I wondered whether the fighting had affected his mind. There were few families untouched by tragedy, including my own. Millions had perished.

Others came back a little crazed.

I'd met way too many in Mr Pritchard's pie-and-mash shop. They were aged beyond their years, broken men who suffered from mental traumas. For the most part, they sat muttering to themselves at a table in the shop and were harmless. The only exception was Peter Thistle.

My voice softened. "A grim time, indeed. It must have been difficult for you."

His head moved in confirmation as he flexed his fingers. "Nothing but dark days and long nights for what seemed like an eternity."

Peter Thistle came back from the war angry and violent, ending his days at the end of the hangman's noose for the murder of an elderly parlour maid.

The man swayed with the rock of the train and cracked his knuckles. "War changes a man, brings out the savage in him."

I glanced at his hands. They looked too small to grasp my neck, but his little arms looked solid, and I knew strength increased in the crazed.

I put on a positive voice, eyes on the alert, body tense. "Every morning brings a fresh start, another day of life to enjoy, don't you think?"

He opened and closed his fingers as if exercising them for some devious purpose. "We shot the cowards, and that was too good for the yellow-bellied buggers. They should've been dispatched with the sword!"

Out of the side of my eye, I noticed the train hallway remained dark and empty. "I suppose the guard will pass by any moment to collect our tickets."

He hesitated, and I waited, watching his long, narrow face, pencil clutched tight in my hand, ready to defend myself should his hands move towards my throat. The train rocked back and forth gently, like a baby's crib.

"Ah!" he cried. "Voting is like hunting or war."

"My, the guard is late in checking our tickets."

"Not everyone enjoys a good hunt or a good war."

"I shall write and complain to the train company."

The little man took off his hat. He turned it round and round in his hands, pinching the crown in and punching it out. Again, he flexed his fingers. "Touch of arthritis, don't you know. Makes the hands stiff, almost useless."

"Oh!" My body relaxed.

"It was not easy being an officer in the war office in London."

"You served in London?"

"It takes nerves of steel to send working-class men to their deaths, but someone had to do it. Caviar and bubbly were in short supply. We had to make do with cod roe and plum wine."

"Goodness, that must have been a challenge."

The man's owl-like eyes narrowed. "If I had my way, I'd take the vote from working men. Why should we let a bunch of uneducated yokels set the direction of our country?"

The polite thing to do would have been to nod and smile and turn my eyes back to my journal. But the man had crept under my skin, his words dancing on a raw nerve. I kept my voice steady and positive. "Surely you don't believe working men who fought for their country have no right to vote?"

The man's eyes darkened, his lower lip turned purple. "Farm-workers here in Norfolk are agitating for higher wages, and when they get in an accident due to their incompetence, they want compensation!"

"Really?"

"It happened again last harvest to a young lad about eighteen years old, I believe. The boy was nothing more than a disreputable, drunken loafer who never did an honest day's work in his life. And now he wants compensation for his own stupidity! Landowners overpay the lazy dogs as it is." He placed the hat on his head and batted the newspaper in his lap as if swatting a fly. "The ballot belongs in the hands of the ruling classes and not the masses—men or women."

Fury boiled in my stomach. The man was positively Victorian in his attitude. My mouth got the better of my judgement. "Are you saying only hereditary lords should have the vote?"

"And the wealthy business class."

We were plunged into sudden darkness as the train entered a tunnel. I let out a quiet gasp, startled by the muffled roar of the wind, the racket of the wheels, and nearness of the blackened brick tunnel walls. Just as quickly, we burst back into the afternoon sunlight and upward along a steep incline with lush, green hills rising all around us.

With only two stops until my destination, I decided to ignore the pompous oaf. I shook my head, chastised myself for choosing an empty carriage, and turned back to my journal.

Chapter 4

"GOVERNESS?"

It was only a single word, but in the man's snooty voice, it seemed to capture, characterise, and belittle all at once. I tried to ignore the question, but I sensed his beady eyes still watching me. I glanced up and caught his cold stare. Annoyed, I said, "Whatever gave you that impression?"

"Ah!" he said as if he'd finished a challenging crossword puzzle. "I am an excellent judge of a person's position in life. And your dress and manner show a degree of refinement. Add to that the lack of a wedding ring, the fact you are riding single in a first-class train carriage, and the answer to the question is almost certain. You are most definitely a governess." He leaned back and smiled, satisfied with his inference. "Which family are you in the employ of?"

My eyes narrowed. "Sir, your powers of deduction need a little work. May I suggest you reread your Sherlock Holmes. *The Hound of the Baskervilles* seems like an apt choice."

There was a pause while the man looked long and hard into my face. "You don't work for a local household?"

"Goodness, you'll next be asking if I till the land with a hoe!"

"And you are not a governess?"

"If that's an offer of employment, the answer is no. I am not in so desperate a need."

He sat very still in his seat, hands on his knees, bent forward as if peering down a microscope. "So how do you spend your day?"

What I did with my day, where I was travelling, and why, were none of his business. "I'm neither a governess nor a servant. My travel to Norfolk is on a matter of personal business."

"Oh, come now, don't take offence." He shifted to the edge of his seat and fixed me with his owl-like stare. "Train travel is expensive, a good thing to keep out the hoi polloi. If you're not in the employ of a wealthy family, I am left to assume you're a woman of independent means?"

If only that were true. With five shillings to my name, I could barely afford the train fare and was grateful Uncle Tristan paid for my ticket. "Sir, you can't expect me to discuss my financial affairs with a stranger."

"Ah! It is not for me to try." His tongue licked the edge of his lips, but there was no mistaking the radiance that lighted up the man's sly face. "Madam, I happen to know of certain gold mines in Peru whose shares you can pick up for next to nothing. Guaranteed to triple in price over the next twelve months, possibly even more."

I said, "Really, sir, I have no interest in the matter."

The train slowed. And stopped.

Bagington Hall!

It was barely a station. A wooden shack set back from a single platform.

The man stood to his feet, removed his hat, and made a low bow. "Sir Richard Sandoe at your service."

My expression shifted from flat-out annoyance to shock. "Sir Richard Sandoe, did you say?"

He fished around in his top pocket, pulled out a small square card, and pressed it into my hand. "Here, this is for you. I'd be happy to help you manage your financial affairs and tell you a bit more about the gold mines in Peru, if you so desire."

He turned to open the carriage door.

I watched him stride from the train and along the platform.

Chapter 5

I SWALLOWED HARD, MY breath catching in my throat, my heart a steady thump against my chest.

"So that was Sir Richard Sandoe!"

I staggered to my feet, hurried to the door, lowered the window, and looked out onto the platform.

But Sir Sandoe was gone.

I slumped back into my seat and with trembling hands unfolded Uncle Tristan's letter. I scanned it with speed, my eyes settling on one line:

You shall start with the Sandoe account—Sir Richard Sandoe and his charming aunt, Lady Louisa Herriman.

How could I face the bigoted little man again, especially since he believed I was an independently wealthy woman?

Beads of sweat bloomed on my forehead. I reread the entire letter.

What could I do?

Oh bother, bother, bother!

I began to think. Ideas came quickly, and with the same rapidity, were found wanting. The first vivid realisation was that my actions might cost my uncle his account. The second was that it might cost me my job. I hadn't yet touched foot in Cromer and might already have sealed the date of my return to London.

Now, Maggie, I told myself, you can find a solution to this. There is a way through this maze. The answer came in a flash—I would persuade Uncle Tristan to assign me to another account. Perhaps one of his clients ran a pie-and-mash shop. He'd understand that I needed to start small, find my feet as it were. Yes, that is what I would do.

"All change!" cried the guard in his dark railway uniform with shiny gold buttons and black cap. "Final stop, Bagington Hall."

I leaned out of the window, waved at the guard, and shouted, "Cromer. I'm going to Cromer."

The guard turned and walked to the carriage door. "What did you say, miss?"

"I have a ticket to Cromer."

"This is Bagington Hall."

"Yes, I know that, but I have a ticket to Cromer."

He tilted his head back, put his hands to his mouth, and yelled, "All change, please. All change."

I stared at the man. Was he crazy? I thought for a moment. Or couldn't he hear properly? Determined to test my theory, I reached for my journal and wrote in large letters:

CROMER. I'M GOING TO CROMER.

He read the note, raised his hat, and scratched his head. "Ole hearing ain't what it used to be. I apologise sincerely, miss, but voices sound like the rumble of the train these days. Cromer?"

I gave a warm smile and an exaggerated nod. "That's right."

"You're on the right train."

"Thank goodness!"

As I paused to crystallise my next thought and write it in the journal, the train guard cut in. "But, miss, you have to get out here and walk to the back. Third class only to Cromer."

Chapter 6

WITH THE GUARD'S HELP, I settled into a third-class compartment. The carriage offered shelter from the elements but little else. It was a barren space with cracked windows clouded with age, and there were ten of us in a space smaller than the first-class carriage.

The guard said, "Not as cosy, miss, but Cromer is only a short ride."

I sat at the end of a bench that would comfortably sit three midgets.

There were five of us.

My arm pressed flush against the carriage door. A cockerel fussed in a crate on the woman's lap next to me. She was a middle-aged dumpling of a woman with a roguish face, bright eager eyes, and tutted at the bird in a husky voice.

"Hullo, luv," said the woman, turning to face me. I'm Mrs Ogbern, lives in Cromer."

I nodded an acknowledgement and tried to keep my nose away from the bird. I love animals but can't have them around me for long. I'm allergic to feathers. They make me sneeze. Same for cats, only worse.

I sneezed. "Hello, nice to meet you, Mrs Ogbern."

Mrs Ogbern peered into my face, long and hard, as if trying to place me. Then she shook her head. "Everyone calls me Hilda."

"I'm Maggie Darling." Again, I sneezed.

"Bird giving you the sniffles, eh? I used to suffer terrible from it. Shame those windows don't open, but it's not a long ride." Hilda dug around in her handbag and pulled out a neatly folded cloth handkerchief. "Here, have this."

Again, I nodded then added a little smile all the while trying to hold back a sneeze.

Directly opposite sat a man in a flat cloth cap, well over sixty with side whiskers, ocean-blue eyes, a pug nose, and a chin as sharp and angular as granite. Next to him, a younger fellow, in the same attire.

The cramped space offered no opportunity for calligraphy, so I half closed my eyes. The journey would be less than twenty minutes.

The engine roared, whistle blasted twice, and the train eased from the station.

"Ay-up, 'ere she goes," said the old man opposite.

I opened my eyes.

The man's lips tugged upward. A tooth stump appeared like an ancient fossil. "Ay-up lass, the name's George Edwards. Me and Frank ain't from around these parts."

"That's Frank Perry," interjected the younger man. "I'm 'ere to find my sweetheart, Tony."

I nodded and smiled and would have paid no further attention, except George pulled out a little brown bag of cobnuts, cracked them with his bare hands, and dropped the shells back into the bag.

Curious how a man with one tooth could possibly eat a cobnut, I'm ashamed to say I stared, unable to take my eyes off the spectacle.

George rolled the kernel in his thick hand, held it under his pug nose, and sniffed. Then I saw the toothless mouth open, the yellow stump exposed like a prehistoric stalactite, kernel flying into the open cavern.

Swiftly his mouth closed.

The bulge of the nut was visible as he rolled it around. First on the left cheek, then the right, the lower lip, followed by the upper. With each rotation around his mouth, it appeared to shrink. Finally, his lips slid back and forth over each other like the sideways motion of a cow chewing its cud. After a minute or two, he spat the soggy remains back into the brown bag.

George nodded in my direction. "Can't chew like I used to, but my taste buds are still strong, and I love a good cobnut."

Embarrassed at my impolite behaviour, I said, "Are you visiting relatives?"

Before he answered, Hilda shoved a meaty elbow into my side. "That's George Edwards, that is. He and Frank are farm union agitators. Ain't that so?"

"Aye, that's me," said George with his toothless smile, "and young Frank is 'ere to help."

Hilda said, "The *Norfolk News* said you were organising in these parts. Wait till I tell my husband, Harold."

George rubbed his chin. "Works the land, does your Harold?"

"Aye," said Hilda. "And the land works him too, harder than an officer barked orders at the soldiers during the war."

George said, "Fought in the war, I did, wasn't a young man when I signed up, either. But I did my duty and survived to tell the tale."

"Not an easy trick," said Hilda. "Only the officers came back in large numbers."

There was a murmur of agreement.

George continued, "When I got back to England, I lived like a beast, worked like a slave, and earned barely enough to put food on the table for my young wife and the little ones."

Another murmur of agreement.

"Thirty-five shillings a week back then to work the land, and the pay ain't changed to this day," said George. "The union's gonna make a strike the likes of which ain't never been seen in these parts."

Hilda said, "Things have been bad for years. Why strike now?"

A thoughtful expression crossed George's face. "You know your gospel, don't you: time and tide wait for no man?"

"Now is our time," added Frank, cracking his knuckles. "We're gonna give the greedy, rich folk a bloody nose."

"I hear," Hilda began, "that the landowners have plans to protect their property."

George almost jumped to his feet. "What landowners? They don't own anything. We come into the world with nothing, and we go out with nothing. Ain't that what the preacher says?"

The train rocked to one side then the other. The cockerel screeched. Hilda steadied the crate. "Well, them that live in the big houses have guns."

"Shan't stop us. We'll shoot first," said Frank.

"Quiet, boy!" barked George. "We'll be 'aving none of that talk, else we'll both swing under the hangman's noose."

The whistle sounded; the train slowed to a crawl.

Hilda lowered her voice. "There was an accident last harvest in the fields of Bagington Hall. Lies a mile from the station we just pulled out of. Sir Richard Sandoe owns the place."

"Bloody toffs," snarled George.

"Don't bite the hand that feeds you!" snapped Hilda. "My Harold works the fields. Without His Lordship's job, I don't know what we'd do—same goes for most in these parts. But the wages haven't been keeping up with the prices, that's for sure. And once you're injured, you're done for."

George rubbed his forearm. "Accidents are part of the farm-workers' load." He held up his left hand; there was nothing but the stump where the little finger once stood. "Lost that to a scythe. Not my fault either; 'twas an accident."

Hilda said, "Oh, that's nothing. Sir Richard Sandoe owns his own machines, not like those poor, small farmers who 'ave to run horses."

"An engine?" said George, unable to hide the admiration in his voice. "As much as I love horses, a good engine will outdo them every time."

"Aye," said Hilda. "But the old horse-drawn contraption didn't take your feet off as easy as a hand snaps a twig. That's what happened to young Tommy Crabapple, only eighteen. The machine took his feet clean off, both of 'em."

"Dear God," I whispered under my breath, not wishing to hear any more.

Hilda continued, "My Harold, a big man, almost passed out at the red and wet and sticky mess splashed onto the stubble."

George said, "What did His Lordship have to say?"

"Sir Sandoe had my Harold and the other men clean up the mess. They gave poor Tommy three shots of brandy and carried him home. Then they got back to work, same day. His Lordship fussed they'd be late gathering up the crops."

George shifted in his seat. "And what of Tommy?"

With a slow shake of the head, Hilda said, "Young Tommy ain't never going to walk no more. He ain't never going to work the fields again either, and round these parts that's all there is."

The whistle sounded: five long blasts as the train pulled into Cromer Station and shuddered to a stop.

On the platform, with a broad smile and his arms waving furiously, was Uncle Tristan.

Chapter 7

UNCLE TRISTAN WAVED his ball-topped cane as he hurried along the platform with quick prancing steps. He wore khaki cord breeches with leather leggings, a striped-peach-and-white shirt open at the neck, a bright orange silk scarf, and a Victorian, black cape thrown across his shoulders.

"Goodness me, could this be my darling niece, Maggie?" he cried in a shrill whistle of delight. "All is now tickety-boo with the world."

We threw our arms about each other and fell into a deep hug. There is nothing like being home with family.

Uncle Tristan said, "Thank God you arrived here safely, my darling niece. To celebrate, here is a little ditty just for you." He cleared his throat, tilted his head towards the heavens, and with a flowery voice, half spoke, half sang:

"Across the stony ridges,
Across the Norfolk plain,
Young Maggie Darling, the pie-and-mash girl,
To Cromer, comes home again."

We both fell about laughing.

"Oh, Uncle, you embellish trivial things as if they were threads of silk," I said, enjoying the fuss.

"My darling Maggie, if only you knew."

"Knew what?" I said, playing the little guessing game.

Uncle Tristan turned to look at the train. "That I have awaited your return, as a dog his master."

"Oh, don't be silly!"

"Dear Maggie, the dark night of winter has turned into day. I feel like a man rescued from a remote island." He threw his arms around me again. "Thank God. Thank God!"

We parted, and with his free hand, he gathered the cape over his skinny knees and danced with the vigour of youth, waving the ball-tipped cane high in the air. Then he twirled around and gave a shout of joy. "Hooray. Young Maggie Darling, the pie-and-mash girl. To Cromer, comes home again. Hooray!"

I remembered my uncle as flamboyant, but this was too much. Other passengers turned to stare in our direction. I gave an embarrassed nod to Hilda Ogbern, a little goodbye wave to George Edwards and young Frank Perry, and a smile to the train guard who raised his hat.

Uncle Tristan tipped his head back and began to sing a popular London music-hall song. "Last week down our alley came a toff. Nice old geezer with a nasty cough... Come on, Maggie, we're celebrating, sing along with me..."

"Oh, Uncle, I can't sing for toffee! If I had to sing for my supper, I'd go hungry."

Uncle Tristan let out a long laugh, stepped back, and surveyed me from head to toe. "In this short interval, darling Maggie," he remarked amiably, "you have put off youth and blossomed into a mature woman. Dear me, how seventeen years have flown by!"

"You look good too, Uncle," I said with delight. But as I took him in, a small doubt crept into my mind. He was painfully thin, somewhat gaunt in the face, and the brightness I remembered that had twinkled like stars in his eyes seemed somehow dimmed.

Then there were his clothes.

His khaki cord breeches were too short in the legs and too baggy around the waist. The cape frayed at the edges, shirt faded, and short in the arms. And there was the silk scarf. I knew it was fashionable once, but that was many years before my birth. It was as if he'd stepped out in the wardrobe of a man who had lived seventy years earlier and a man with much shorter arms and legs at that.

Uncle Tristan must have seen the questioning look in my eyes, for he said, "Do you remember Mr Gunthorpe?"

"The old man who lived in Belham Cottage?"

"That's right. His mother was from Austria, high up in the mountains. She used to dress him in short trousers and wooden clogs year-round, stunted his growth, I reckon. The poor fellow died last February."

Saddened at the passing of the old man, I said, "When I was a child, I thought he was the oldest person in the world."

"He was ninety-eight and left four shillings and two pence in the Post Office Savings Bank, and was, thus, buried by the parish."

I said, "Oh, I'm sorry. That's not the most dignified send-off for a cornerstone of our community."

Uncle said, "Not to worry, the new vicar, Wilfred Humberstone, did a wonderful service and afterwards gave me Mr Gunthorpe's clothes. Everything I'm wearing, except the silk scarf."

A little spiderweb of concern crept into my mind. Sharing clothes of the deceased was common amongst the poor in London. The police were often called to break up fights between relatives over little more than rags. But I had always presumed Uncle Tristan to be well off, for he had lived a life of artistic adventure, and I was never aware of money in his presence.

I said, "Oh, Uncle, it was kind of you to accept the vicar's gift... but do you feel you have to wear the clothes without having them tailored?"

He waved the question away with a rather theatrical flourish. "Not a perfect fit, I'll give you that. But it would be disrespectful to Mr Gunthorpe's memory not to wear them as he intended."

I thought back to when Father bought the mangle for Nancy and sensed there was more to it. With a casual air to my voice, I said, "How is the business going?"

There was a moment of silence as Uncle Tristan tapped his cane on the wooden slats of the platform as if assessing its strength. "Dearest Maggie, we shall discuss such things tomorrow. Now let's get you over to Mrs Rusbridger's wonderful lodgings before nightfall."

Chapter 8

IT WAS DARK WHEN WE arrived at Mrs Rusbridger's boarding house. Overhead, the moon was a gorgeous buttery lantern in a greyish-purple sky. Only the faint noise of waves crashing on the nearby shore, the wistful wind in the trees overhead, and our footsteps on the gravel driveway broke the silence.

The house was built of rough grey-green stone. Clematis and tea roses grew along wooden trellises attached to the wall. The large leaded windows, with big oak beams that angled across the wide walls, gave the building a distinctive rustic look. A solitary oil lamp illuminated the entranceway. Uncle Tristan and I watched the shadows creep and dance in its flickering light.

"I remember this place," I said, looking around. "It used to be the King's Head Tavern."

"Ah, yes," said Uncle Tristan in a voice brimming with nostalgia. "Your father spent many a lazy Sunday afternoon in the old establishment. I, too, participated in their fine ales and meat pies as I thought up new poetic sonnets."

"When did it close down?"

"Years ago. We locals still refer to it as The Tavern, but the building lay abandoned for at least a decade. Lord Blackwood gave the property to his wife as a gift about three years ago. Lady Blackwood is a bit of a social reformer, and she turned it into a"—he paused as if searching for the words—"Victorian-style, ladies-only boarding house, and hired Mrs Rusbridger to run the place. It is a delightful guest house that conjures up a bygone era, with prices to match."

I'd seen remnants of Victorian accommodations in London. They still called them fourpenny dosshouses. In their grimy brick walls, the poor and desperate found room and board for a few coppers. I sucked in a deep breath as I recalled reading about a squabble between vagrants over a frying pan. They set the building alight, and everyone perished in the inferno.

"Uncle, are you sure this is a respectable establishment?"

"Lady Blackwood is a paragon of virtue, a pillar of our community, and as for Mrs Rusbridger, she is a no-nonsense woman, and a dear friend. When one is in need, she always comes through." Uncle Tristan knocked on the door with his cane. "Maggie, I'd have you stay at my lodgings, but I fear they are insufficient for your needs."

The front door creaked open. A tall, plump woman with a round face and saucers for eyes, peered out. She was around six feet in height with arms as thick as tree trunks. A mop of curly, grey hair peeked from under a ragged headscarf. "Yes?"

"Greetings, Mrs Rusbridger." Uncle Tristan gave a deep bow. "It is I, Mr Harbottle, with my niece, Maggie Darling."

Mrs Rusbridger opened the door wide and stepped onto the little porch. The night air filled with the fumes of cheap brandy. "Yes," she said again, this time adding a slight nod in my direction.

Uncle repeated his greeting. "It is I, Mr Harbottle, come with Maggie Darling, from London, to reside in your humble abode."

Her sharp green eyes blinked. "Yes."

Uncle Tristan stepped forward. The gentle glow of the lamp illuminated the concern that crossed his face. He tried again, "Miss Darling's room is ready, is it not?"

The woman placed a thick hand on her chin. She swayed from side to side for a moment, then her eyes narrowed. "Room?"

The single word knocked Uncle Tristan off his stride. He stumbled two steps back into the flickering shadows. "The lodgings we discussed for my dearest niece. She is here, down from London this very evening."

Mrs Rusbridger shook her head. "Mr Harbottle, I don't recall you booking a room." There was a heavy emphasis on the word booking.

"We discussed it, not four weeks ago," protested Uncle Tristan.

Again, Mrs Rusbridger shook her head. "Are you sure you made the booking?" Once again, there was a rather unusual emphasis on the last word.

The penny appeared to drop. Uncle Tristan fished around in the pockets of his Victorian cape. "Will two pennies be sufficient to secure entrance to your esteemed establishment?"

"Four."

Uncle eyed Mrs Rusbridger with the look of a wounded puppy. "Very well."

Mrs Rusbridger's thick hands grasped the coins. "I have a room at the back; that will 'ave to do. It's where my brother, Alan, died." She turned, and we followed her inside. "I've kept it just as it were when he was alive. Don't mind the mice, could do with another cat around here. Those little pests have been taking liberties since old Hoppy died. He were a good moggy."

The dark, narrow hallway smelled of lamp oil and bacon grease. A sudden pang of hunger cast my thoughts back to my uncle's letter.

We shall celebrate your arrival with a feast. Only the best Norfolk offers for my wonderful niece!

I inhaled hoping to catch the scent of something roasting on the fire. But no odour of a hearty roast filled my nostrils. No stewed vegetables, not even the faintest trace of steam from boiling water.

As if reading my thoughts, Uncle Tristan said, "Maggie, a plate of supper is in order. How about a large bowl of mulligatawny soup followed by three thick slices of roast beef, gravy, mustard, pickles, with a side of boiled cabbage?"

My stomach rumbled in agreement. "Delightful, that would go down a real treat."

Uncle Tristan said, "Mrs Rusbridger, can you rustle that up for Maggie, and I shall have a small plate of sardines with Gorgonzola cheese."

Mrs Rusbridger's head half turned. "Bread and lard is all we got."

Uncle Tristan waved his ball-tipped cane in annoyance. "Bread and lard!"

Mrs Rusbridger met him with a stony stare. "For four pennies, it's bread and lard or nothing."

"Tickety-boo," said Uncle with haste. "All that bread will remind our Maggie of her father in London. He's in the bakery business, you know, making a pretty penny in our capital city."

Mrs Rusbridger's oval eyes seemed to widen at the mention of money. "A killing in bakery goods?"

"Yes, yes. There are millions of hungry people in London. Bakeries can hardly keep up with the clamour for bread. Maggie's father is raking in the king's currency faster than you can crack an egg. Maggie will be your finest guest; her father would have it no other way." Uncle Tristan raised the ball-tipped cane to his head in a salute. "Are you sure you can't rustle up a stray tin of sardines?"

Mrs Rusbridger said, "I'll warm up some water for a pot of tea."

Uncle Tristan, the eternal optimist, replied, "To go with our sardines and Gorgonzola cheese?"

Mrs Rusbridger let out a savage grunt. "Now just you—"

"Bread and lard is wonderful," I said, interrupting. It was better than nothing. "A simple supper after a long journey is all one really needs."

The large woman turned, patted down a stray curl of hair, and for the first time, I saw the flicker of a smile across her face. "There is a quarter jug of milk in the larder, I'll add a splash with a little sugar to your tea and a nice dollop of brandy to warm your bones. As for you, Mr Harbottle, if you want to dine, that'll be four pennies."

Uncle Tristan beat a hasty retreat. "Maggie, you are in safe hands. Let us meet tomorrow at my business premises. It's on the town square, the top floor of John and Sons butcher shop. How does noon sound?"

"Isn't that a little late?" I was used to rising at 4 a.m.

"Nothing happens in Cromer before noon and even less at Tristan's Hands. Let's give the birds a chance to wake up and sing. Enjoy your supper. See you tomorrow."

Chapter 9

THE FOLLOWING MORNING found me in good spirits. I had enjoyed a good night's sleep. I washed with cold water and put on a tailored tweed skirt, cotton blouse, and jacket. I wanted to look professional on my first day at Uncle Tristan's office.

In the kitchen, I enjoyed a good chat with Mrs Rusbridger along with a hearty breakfast of eggs, ham with bread, and tea. We talked about the bakery business, London, and she even shared that I was one of only three guests.

"The other ladies left at dawn for Norwich," she said. "So I packed 'em boiled eggs, cheese, pickles, and bread. Go on, 'ave another slice of ham. That's wild hog, caught by the new vicar over at Bagington Hall."

It was, therefore, with a full stomach and high spirits, I left the boarding house.

The gentle morning sun shone from a cloudless, blue sky as I strolled along the lane into the village. I had a full hour before noon and my meeting with Uncle Tristan. Although it had been seventeen years, the village had not changed a great deal, except many of the dirt tracks were now paved.

At the iron gates of Saint Magdalene, I stopped, adjusted my hair, and followed the rose-bush-lined flagstone path that led to the cemetery. I ambled amongst the oak trees and the graves, stopping here and there to read the headstones. I found the resting place of Mr Gunthorpe and paid my respects in quiet prayer.

With heavy steps, I turned towards a distant shaded area. My heartbeat quickened, and my mood became sombre. Walking more deliberately, I approached a clump of shrubs, beyond which lay, in the shade of an old oak tree, a single headstone.

I stopped at my mother's grave.

The land sloped gently away to a rocky stream. The rustle of water over the stones drifted faintly in the air with the musical tinkle of raindrops on a glass windowpane. Beyond the walled graveyard were hedgerows lit here and there by the mid-morning sun. The spot was all so rural and still.

A beautiful resting place for Mother.

As I stooped to clear away weeds at the base of the headstone, I saw a small china vase filled with wilted, brown roses. There was a little yellowed card at the side. I picked it up.

Scrawled in a thin, untidy hand were the words:

Miss you, big sister.

Tristan.

Tears rolled down my cheeks.

"Miss you too, Mother. So does Father and little Nancy."

A sharp scuffling came from behind.

I spun around, expecting to see a rabbit or fox.

Nothing.

Standing very still, I scanned the tombstones, rosebushes, and oak trees.

Still nothing.

"Missed it!"

I half turned back towards my mother's tombstone, when, from the corner of my eye, a shadow flickered.

This time I spun around with speed.

The sun went behind a cloud, casting shadows across the tombstones. A figure, all in black, darted between the shrubs and crouched down low beside a statue.

There was a rapid whoosh of air followed by a high-pitched squeal. The figure stood up and hurried in my direction.

It was a man.

He carried a bow with a quiver filled with arrows slung across his shoulder.

And he was smiling.

"Wilfred Humberstone." He adjusted his dog collar. "I'm the new vicar."

He was a short, thickset man in his sixties, with a large nose, heavy moustache, ruddy complexion, and bright, piercing eyes.

With a half curtsy, half bow, I said, "Maggie Darling, nice to meet you."

The vicar beamed and encased my hand in strong, rough, calloused fingers. They felt more like those of a working man than an office-bound priest. Instantly, I warmed to Vicar Humberstone.

"Maggie Darling," said the vicar, rolling the words around his mouth as if savouring a fine wine. "Ah, yes, Mr Harbottle's niece. Your uncle has had a rum time of things. Are you down from London to stay?"

I should have answered with a question like "What on earth were you doing crouching behind headstones with a bow and arrow?" or "Tell me more about Uncle Tristan's problems." But his natural smile and soft voice threw me off. I said, "I've come down to help with my uncle's business."

The vicar's eyes dropped to the headstone. "And to visit your mother."

A sob caught in my throat. I nodded and said, "Seventeen years since Mother left us."

The vicar touched my shoulder. "Dear, your Uncle Tristan told me all about her. She sounded like a wonderful person. I would have loved to have met her."

Together, we stood in silence under the branches of the oak tree. Birds chirped. The breeze rustled through the leaves.

After a long moment, the vicar pulled out a silver hip flask, took a quick sip, then said, "Medicinal purposes. The doctor says it keeps the airways clear." He nodded towards the bow. "Old fashioned, I know. The wife overfeeds the vicarage cats. I use the bow and arrows to keep the rats down. Much better than shooting. The only downside is the cunning rodents make a terrible racket when you miss 'em."

I laughed then said, "Sounded like a soul screaming from hell."

Again, the vicar chuckled. "That's a clever way of putting it. The bow and arrow are my little pastime. I enjoy it for hunting too: more natural than a gun. The sound of an arrow attracts less attention than the sharp crack of a bullet."

"I can't say I really see the difference, at least for the rat."

"Well, it really comes into play when I'm hunting pheasant or game in the grounds of Bagington Hall. West Wood is the best spot for that. Nice and quiet. A gun would make a terrible racket and alert the gamekeeper..." His face flushed. He'd said more than he intended. "Not that I endorse poaching, but there's nothing quite like braised pheasant with roast potatoes and apple sauce for Sunday afternoon dinner, is there?"

Chapter 10

TRISTAN'S HANDS WAS through John and Sons butcher shop, up a narrow flight of stairs, at the end of a short corridor. It was a small loft with a tiny window, bare wooden floors, and exposed brick wall. The air hung with a thick, unidentifiable stench.

Uncle Tristan sat behind a wooden writing desk. A spider plant struggled for life in a small pot on one corner, a leather briefcase on the other. His cape hung across the back of his chair. He wore the outfit of the previous evening, the only difference being the shadow of stubble across his chin and the ruffled, unkempt nature of his hair.

"Welcome, dearest Maggie," he said, rising to his feet. "Enter the beating heart of the Harbottle commercial enterprise." He pranced light footed in front of his desk, pulled up a chair, and said, "Take a seat; we've got work to do."

I sat down, sniffed, covered my nose, and said, "What's that loathsome smell?"

"They cure hides in a shack at the back of the butchers. Alas, the unsavoury aroma seems to drift up here where it multiplies in intensity. It's not so bad when you get used to it."

I removed my hand from my nose. "How long does that take?"

A particular noxious stench wafted into the room. Uncle Tristan paled, covered his mouth, and coughed. "Ah, well, as you can see, I'm still adjusting."

When Uncle Tristan wrote for me to come to Cromer, I'd had visions of working in an office with great glass windows that looked out onto Norfolk scenery. A tiny windowed loft at the top of a butcher shop wasn't what I was expecting nor the foul smell from curing hides.

I said, "Uncle, how long have you been here?"

Uncle Tristan ignored the question and pointed to a small writing bureau crammed up against the brick wall. "Maggie, that's your workspace."

The view was of the dust-ridden brick wall with cobwebs in the corners.

Now the faint trace of concern from Vicar Humberstone's earlier words were combined with the shabby sight of my uncle and the stench of the office. It grew like a snowball gathers ice as it rolls down a hill. This was definitely not what I expected.

I said, "No, this will never do. At least the prisoner glancing up through the bars can see a little of the daytime sky."

"It's only until we move to more suitable accommodation."

"When is that?"

He raised a hand. "How much were they paying you in the pie-and-mash shop?"

"Twenty-five shillings a week."

"Then I'll pay you fifty!"

"Are you sure?"

Uncle leaned across the desk and took my hands in his. "Oh, yes, Maggie. I know you want to bring Nancy home—your mother would want that. But you'll need money."

"You want to bring Nancy home to Cromer too, don't you?"

Uncle turned away. "Nancy is not my child. It is not for me to say, but her mother would have wished it so."

I glanced around the space. There were no filing cabinets, no hanging files, no stacks of papers strewn about the desk. Not even a typewriter. There was nothing at all to suggest a working office.

My mind went back to Mr Pritchard who always said, "You can have the world's best pie-and-mash shop, but if it is in the Sahara Desert, it will soon close."

I said, "Uncle, is the business profitable?"

"Oh, yes, very profitable."

I glanced around. The bare brick walls, exposed wooden floors, and lack of furniture told a different story.

"Are you sure?"

"Oh, dearest Maggie, it is not as it seems."

"Really?"

Uncle leaned back in his chair and placed his feet on the desk. "You know I'm wearing Mr Gunthorpe's clothes. Alas, I have no others."

I'd suspected as much, but nonetheless, his candid admission shocked me. Then it struck me—I'd left London to work for my dear uncle who couldn't afford to put clothes on his own back. In a blind panic, I cried, "No!"

"And I'm living in a shed—"

I felt dizzy. "Dear God!"

"At the bottom of Mrs Banbury's garden. She's a patron of Saint Magdalene and good friends with the vicar's wife."

My throat went dry. "A shed at the bottom of a garden?"

"By the vegetable patch."

I swallowed hard, regretting for the first time leaving Mr Pritchard's pie-and-mash shop. "Tell me it isn't so, Uncle."

Uncle Tristan burst out in fits of wild laughter. He was barely able to get the next sentence out. "And I bathe in the river!"

"Uncle," I said in a stern voice, "you jest!"

"Every word I've spoken is perfectly true."

And from his tone and manner, I knew that it was.

"But, Uncle, why are you living in a shed? Why are you wearing a dead man's clothes? And how can you afford to pay me fifty shillings a week?"

Uncle stood. "Aren't you worth fifty shillings a week?"

"It is rather a lot, but—"

"But nothing. Nancy is worth a hundred shillings a week, and so are you!"

"Have you finally let slip the reins of sanity?" Not for the first time, I wondered if my uncle hadn't gone completely mad. "This is crazy talk."

Uncle Tristan sat down and rocked back and forth with laughter. "When I worked in the circus, I made a pretty packet. Saved most of it too. They called me Lord Avalon, Man of Mystery. The crowds flocked to see my illusions. I'd hoped one day to break into the big time like John Maskelyne."

I said, "I'd heard he used to perform in London."

"He was the greatest Victorian stage magician." Uncle paused, closed his eyes, and said, "Alas, for me, fame never materialised, and I gave up the profession. But I knew one day my chance to become rich would arrive. I've waited and waited, and now at last my turn has come."

Again, I glanced about the tiny room trying to make sense of his words. "Are you talking about Tristan's Hands?"

"No. Tristan's Hands is my latest venture." His eyes opened very wide. "There is one before it, one which shall reward me handsomely and very soon."

Intrigued, I said, "What other venture?"

Uncle got up and hurried towards the door. Satisfied there was no one listening in the corridor, he returned to his desk and lowered his voice to a whisper. "Maggie, I've invested everything I own to buy shares of a gold mine in Peru. I got the tip from a client. I believe I wrote to you about him, Sir Richard Sandoe?"

Chapter 11

UNCLE TRISTAN WAS ON his feet, prancing with quick little steps back and forth across the tiny room.

"I first met Sir Sandoe at the Norwich horse races: a rather unusual man, small with the long face of a mule. It was he who gave me the idea for Tristan's Hands, and later when he saw it excited me, mentioned the gold mine in the jungles of Peru."

The thought of Uncle Tristan betting everything on a gold mine in a distant land caused my stomach to churn. Didn't he know not to put every egg in a single basket?

I opened my mouth to speak then closed it again. Uncle Tristan was extreme by nature, and after all, was this not the great opportunity he'd waited all his adult life for? What right did I have to tell him not to take the chance?

Uncle Tristan said, "If I could, I'd sell Mr Gunthorpe's clothes and walk about naked!" He stopped and placed a hand to his cheek as if considering the possibility. Then he returned to his frenetic pacing. "But decency wouldn't allow it, and of course, I've put a little aside for the running of my motor vehicle, food, and the like. But not a penny for the clothes on my back!"

"Well," I said, "at least you haven't totally lost your mind."

He tapped a finger at the side of his head. "Maggie, it is all there. What does it matter being without fine garments and housing for just a short while? Sir Sandoe expects word of a great discovery before the year is out. Then I shall buy myself a wardrobe fit for a king."

Again, I opened my mouth to sound a warning, but I clamped it shut. If I had more than five shillings in my purse, I, too, would grab Sir Sandoe's shares and use the money to bring Nancy from London. Then I'd visit Sharrington Insane Asylum and buy the freedom of Antoinette Sandoe.

I said, "Are all the shares sold?"

Uncle Tristan was still pacing back and forth. "When news breaks, there'll be an unholy dash to buy." He stopped by the door, opened it, and peered out into the corridor. Then he closed it and leaned his back against the wood and smiled. "That's when I shall sell! Oh, darling Maggie, soon your uncle will be a millionaire."

The wheels whirred in my brain, trying to take it all in. "A millionaire?"

"Well, maybe not. But I will be rich, and if the mad dash to grab the stock is strong enough, who knows? That is why Sir Sandoe has sworn me to secrecy."

"But you told me?"

"So you can invest as well. I'm going to write to your father." Uncle Tristan danced on the spot. "Soon, we all shall be rich."

"Uncle, I only have five shillings to my name."

Uncle Tristan stopped his merry jig, stared at me for a long moment, then said, "If you had more, would you invest?"

"Oh, yes!"

"I'm paying you fifty shillings a week, aren't I? Take an advance from the next year's wages and use that." He twirled around in a circle kicking his legs high in the air like a French cabaret performer. "Come, Maggie, let's dance."

Before I could protest, he swept me up in his skinny arms, and we twirled around the tiny room. "Last week, down our alley, came a toff. Nice old geezer with a nasty cough..."

At last he stopped, doubled over to catch his breath, beads of sweat running down his forehead.

"Maggie, all is tickety-boo in the world."

As my heartbeat slowed, practicality kicked in. "Uncle, will your clients advance you my wages?"

"They will," he huffed. "It is but mere blackbird scratchings from their purse. I have only to ask. If you wish, I shall invest the advance on your behalf."

Peru was a long way from Cromer, and I knew nothing of gold mining, but an opportunity presented itself, and after a life of toil and grief, I would take it.

"Keep back fifteen shillings a week. I'll need that for living expenses."

Uncle Tristan touched his forelock in the dramatic manner of an actor in a London theatre. "As you wish, madam."

It was then I thought of Sir Richard Sandoe. I couldn't risk meeting the man, not yet, anyway. I had to persuade Uncle Tristan to assign me to another account. "How many clients do you have?"

"Let me see." His eyes narrowed. "Now, what a question."

"Uncle, how many?"

He raised the fingers of his right hand and counted like a child. Then he looked up, eyes blank. "Right now?"

"Yes."

"One. The Sandoe account."

"Are there no others?"

"Lady Blackwood expressed an interest, but I've heard nothing."

My heart sank like a stone tossed into a well. "Oh bother!"

"No bother at all. One fat-pursed client is better than none." Uncle sat down at the desk. "Lady Herriman is in charge of staffing. She makes all the decisions: doubt we'll need to bother Sir Sandoe. He is a busy man."

Uncle's words lifted my mood. Sir Sandoe ran a large estate with an army of servants and helpers, and I was to work as Uncle's bookkeeper in this stench-ridden office. What was the chance we'd meet again? And even if we did, such an encounter might be weeks or even months away. With time, the memory fades. He might not even recognise me.

Now I knew I could do this.

Everything would work out just fine.

"Very well," I said, "Let me familiarise myself with the account. Where are the books?"

Uncle scratched his head. "Well, er, you see, the account is new." He reached for the briefcase and pulled out a bundle of papers. "The details are here. Can you tootle over to Bagington Hall with these documents? Lady Herriman is expecting you at three."

Chapter 12

A RAY OF SUN SHONE through the tiny window, casting a hazy beam into Uncle Tristan's office at the top floor of John and Sons butchers.

"We shall drive to Bagington Hall. Once there, Lady Herriman will receive you." Uncle Tristan spoke fast as if fearful I might see something distasteful between the gaps in his words. "Everything has been carefully worked out and arranged."

The thought of meeting a real-life lady left me nervous. As the sun ducked behind a cloud, and the gloom returned to the room, I said, "Should I curtsy when I meet Her Ladyship?"

"It can't hurt. See if you can throw in a bow as well. And don't forget to doff your cloche hat."

"Uncle! Be serious. I don't want to make a mistake and let you down." Nor did I want to run into Sir Sandoe, but I kept quiet on that.

"Maggie, you worked in a pie-and-mash shop; you can handle Lady Herriman."

An image of the elongated donkey face and owl-like stare of Sir Sandoe came to mind. "But what is she like?"

"In looks, nothing like Sir Sandoe, different family line, and her character..." Uncle Tristan grinned like a Cheshire cat. "In your letters, you mentioned Mr Pritchard. Well, I suppose he has a lot in common with Lady Herriman."

"How so?"

"They both like to lord it over people."

"That's it." I stamped my foot. "When we meet, I shan't say a word, just follow your lead."

"Maggie, I won't be with you."

"Eh?"

A waft of putrid air filled the room.

Uncle coughed. It was a little too long, a little too hard. Then he waved his right arm about, like a London policeman directing traffic. And that was a little too theatrical.

Something was wrong, and I wanted to know what.

"Now listen here," I said, "Maggie Darling wasn't born yesterday. What is going on?"

"Just like your mother," Uncle said in a soft voice. "It is quite simple. You are to give Her Ladyship the documents. Then she will dismiss you."

"If that is all I have to do, why won't you be with me?"

"I shall remain in the carriage house, with Boots."

"Who?"

"Boots is a kind of footman. The carriage house acts as a garage for motor vehicles these days. Lady Herriman is rather particular with the titles of household staff. Dolly Trimmings is Her Ladyship's chambermaid."

"How very Victorian!"

"Ah, yes, remnants of that time still exist. While you meet with Her Ladyship, I shall remain at a safe distance in the carriage house. I must speak with Boots and other staff. After all, Tristan's Hands needs a list of workers for when it gains new clients. No matter how genial the landowner, there are always one or two unhappy fellows on staff."

"How about I remain with Boots, and you visit with Lady Herriman?"

"Alas, that is impossible."

"Why?"

"Lady Herriman is rather a challenging woman."

"Uncle, you worked in the circus."

He put on his best American accent, face twisted as if he'd sucked on a lemon. "Ain't nobody can tame that lioness. Anyway, she refuses to see me."

"Uncle, what did you do?"

"Nothing."

"If I am to meet with Her Ladyship, I must have a clear head. How can I do that if my mind is filled with what you might have done to offend the poor woman?"

"Ah, your logic makes perfect sense, but I have done nothing."

"Nothing?"

"That's right. If you want to blame anything, blame the passage of time."

"What are you talking about?"

"Maggie, I am considerably older than when we last met."

"Uncle, you've hardly changed, apart from losing a bit of weight, and your sense of fashion may be a little outdated."

"And neither have you changed, my dearest niece. If anything, you appear younger. It is quite remarkable."

Uncle Tristan knew how to flatter.

"Thank you. I feel no older than thirty."

"Seventeen at most, with a good corset."

I giggled. "Oh, do you think so? That is so kind."

Uncle Tristan continued, "Lady Herriman says I remind her too much of the nineteen twenties."

"But this is nineteen twenty-three!"

"Her Ladyship has rather conservative sensibilities." Uncle Tristan let out a sigh. "I thought Mr Gunthorpe's Victorian cape would help. But no, Lady Herriman refuses to see me. I am too colourful for her tastes."

I glanced at his striped-peach-and-white shirt open at the neck, and bright orange silk scarf. "I can't see why Her Ladyship should think that."

Uncle jumped to his feet, pointed a finger, and said, "Maggie, you were never a good liar. Anyway, I'm banned from an audience with Her Ladyship. Fortunately, Sir Sandoe insists she uses my company for new staff. That is where you come in."

A sinking feeling filled my stomach. I could sense one of Uncle's plans coming on. "Please explain."

Uncle Tristan sat down. "Lady Herriman has a fascination with youth."

"What's unusual about that? She is a lady. I imagine she surrounds herself with pearls and diamonds and beautiful objects."

Uncle Tristan let go another cough, this time both hands waved in the air. "Well... er... yes."

I said, "What is it?"

"I let her know I have a pretty, young assistant, barely out of secretarial school, from a sophisticated borough in London, working as my clerk." Uncle Tristan turned to stare me in the eye. "That would be you, Maggie."

Aghast, I said, "I'm forty-two!"

"You were twenty-five when we last met and young for your age."

"My God, Uncle, you've gone too far this time. How on earth can I pass for a girl in the first blossom of her youth?"

"Have you no powder, no rouge, no imagination?"

"It won't work. I'm a pie-and-mash-shop woman with a figure to match!"

He folded his arms. "Then how shall we get the money for your advance?"

I had no answer to that.

Uncle Tristan's voice dropped to a soft whisper. "A dab of powder here and there will work wonders." Before I could protest, his lips twisted into the grin of a fox that had discovered a secret entrance to the henhouse. "Lady Herriman greets visitors in a darkened room. I've asked Dolly Trimmings, her chambermaid, to hide Her Ladyship's lorgnette spectacles. She won't be able to see a thing."

"Uncle!"

"All you have to do is keep your distance and giggle a little here and there. Now why don't you go back to Mrs Rusbridger's boarding house, slap on some makeup, and I'll pick you up at a quarter to two."

Chapter 13

THE SKY WAS BRIGHT blue with immense silvery clouds when we approached the gatehouse of Bagington Hall. There were table-cloths spread on long wooden benches; red, white, and blue bunting; and flags fluttered at the tops of long poles. Women in summer frocks, with bonnets perched on their heads, handed out plates of food. Small children played on the green grass that led to the high stone wall of the estate.

Uncle Tristan pulled over to the verge and parked.

"Maggie, come on; they are having a picnic. Let's grab a bite. I've had nothing but a crust of dry bread, a couple of carrots from the vegetable plot, and a cup of tea since morning."

I said, "We are not guests. Do we even have time?"

But Uncle Tristan took off, prancing in long strides towards the gathered crowd.

As I hurried behind, I gazed at the gatehouse. In front of the iron gates, men on bicycles rode in a tight circle. They wore heavy black boots; shabby, grey, flannel trousers; patched jackets, with flat cloth caps—the unofficial uniform of farmhands.

To one side on a soapbox, with a megaphone in hand, stood a stooped man with a sharp, angular face covered with side whiskers. I recognised him at once—George Edwards. At his side, puffing on a clay pipe, was young Frank Perry. Even through the grey-blue haze of smoke, I could sense tension to his form, like a coil about to explode.

George turned in my direction, raised his cloth cap, then gave a little wave.

I waved back.

"Ay-up," began George, placing a megaphone to his lips. "This is an official union strike. There'll be no harvesting or farm work by union members today. Only exception is the Blackwood Estate, cos they treat their staff right."

A cheer went up from the gathered crowd.

"As for them in London, and the Minister of Agriculture. I say we'll not back down! Fair pay, fair work conditions, and we'll give you a fair day's work!"

Another cheer went up from the crowd.

"Now we 'ave plenty of food and drink. Eat and enjoy."

This comment raised the most tremendous cheer. The men parked their bicycles and headed for the tables.

I joined the line that served potato salad, roast chicken, bread, and pickles with a tankard of apple cider. I looked around for Uncle Tristan, but he was nowhere to be seen, so I sat at a table to eat on my own. The cider was strong and good. I drank it in several large gulps.

"Miss Darling, fancy meeting you again today. Good on you grabbing a tankard of the local brew before they run out. It is potent stuff; take it easy."

I glanced up to see the smiling face of Vicar Humberstone. In one hand, he held a large drumstick, in the other, a tankard of cider. Over his shoulder, he carried his bow and a quiver full of arrows.

"Roast turkey," he said, waving the drumstick. "They rear them in Norfolk, you know: the Matthews Estate, over in Sharrington. They make a pretty penny selling the birds in London."

I said, "Isn't that where they have the insane asylum?"

Vicar Humberstone took a long drink. "Aye, that was a dreadful institution. It lingers over the village like a bad fog. The only good thing I can say about the place is that they kept it open until the last inmate died."

Curious, I said, "When was it closed?"

Vicar Humberstone glanced towards the stone wall. "It must be over twenty years by now."

"Are you sure?"

"Absolutely. I was the vicar of Saint Mary's in Sharrington for ten of those years. That required me to work as the chaplain for the asylum." He took a gulp from his tankard. "I wrote a pamphlet on the history of the institution. The last patient was admitted in eighteen hundred and eighty-four. It only took men. When he died, they closed the place down."

A truck trundled along the lane, its loud engine cutting into our conversation like an angry bear. Suddenly men were on their bicycles, a little circle of humanity forming a wall in front of Bagington Hall gates.

The truck shuddered to a stop in front of the pickets. The engine purred.

"Let 'em pass," bellowed George into the megaphone. "We are 'ere to protest peacefully. We'll not let violence touch our protest."

The men drew back.

As the gate swung open, the truck lurched forward. It was then I saw Frank Perry, clinging flat against the back doors.

At the gatehouse, the truck stopped. The gatekeeper came out of his brick hut. He was a long, barrel-chested man; clean shaven; wearing an old hunting coat; a pair of shabby, brown, flannel trousers; and thick, black boots. He saw Frank and gave an angry shout.

Frank jumped off the truck. The gatekeeper approached, his face purple with rage. They were a body length apart, eyes locked, bodies rigid. Frank crouched, reached into his pocket; there was a flash of silver. By now, men poured from the gatehouse. To my surprise, Uncle Tristan was amongst them, his eyes bright with excitement.

The gatekeeper's men surrounded Frank then advanced. There was a brief struggle. Frank twisted and turned then collapsed to the floor. The men dragged him like a sack of potatoes back through the gates, dumping him at the feet of George Edwards.

Now everyone was watching. A crowd of people gathered around, keeping a distance from the gatekeeper and his men.

"Any more of that nonsense, and I'll 'ave the police out here," said the gatekeeper, waving a fist at Frank.

"Do that," growled Frank. "Call 'em." He clambered to his feet and sprung towards the gatekeeper. But he was a big man and effortlessly deflected Frank's advance.

George raised his hands, palms out. "Frank, we'll 'ave none of that nonsense. We are 'ere to peaceable protest."

"Don't look like that to me," replied the gatekeeper. "I'll 'ave to 'ave the police out now for sure."

At that moment, a shadow flickered in the corner of my eye. I turned away from the scuffle to see a figure in black scaling the stone wall—Vicar Humberstone. He took a quick darting glance towards the crowd, his eyes shining with savage pleasure.

Chapter 14

"A RATHER UNFORTUNATE blemish on a rather splendid picnic." Uncle pulled the motorcar to a stop by the carriage house at the side of the main building and let out a drunken laugh. "Imagine running out of the local brew just as things were getting going. Damn disgrace."

There was a heavy sweet odour of cider about him. I'd downed a full tankard myself. It had been a while since I'd tasted farmbrewed, fermented apples, and I knew by the buzz in my head, I must build up my tolerance to their alcoholic content.

I said, "It's Frank Perry I feel sorry for. They hauled him about like a sack of coal. What was he doing riding on the back of the truck?"

Uncle Tristan seemed to sober for a moment. "Maggie, local feelings are running high. Pay and work conditions and all of that. Ah, here is Boots."

A weedy, undersized young man, about nineteen, with a round head and a long, pale, swanlike neck hurried from the building. His eyes were tiny slits in a pasty-white face.

"How is you, Mr Harbottle; enjoying the fine weather?"

"Indeed I am," replied Uncle, giving Boots the keys. "And I have my niece with me today, just a slip of a lass barely out of childhood."

He touched his forelock in that overly dramatic way of his. "I present you, the young Miss Maggie Darling."

I could have kicked Uncle but smiled sweetly as the world swayed around. A tankard of cider was a little too much, and with the afternoon sun, I felt a little dizzy. "Nice to meet you, Boots," I said then gave a little giggle.

"That's it," Uncle Tristan whispered. "But save it until you meet Her Ladyship."

Boots scratched his head. "Aye, delighted to meet you, Miss Darling. Just left school, you say?"

"Fresh as a blackbird's morning song," said Uncle Tristan. "And down from London last Sunday."

"Uncle, please!"

But there was no stopping the man once he got going.

"No doubt our Maggie will have the young men of Norfolk flinging themselves at her like wild bees at the first flower of spring." He paused, stared the young man directly in the eyes, and asked, "Are you walking out with a lady, Boots?"

The man's long neck flushed; his narrow eyes grew wide. "Well... er... yes... I shall propose this very weekend, sir."

Uncle waved his hands in mock frustration and let out an exaggerated sigh. "Well, Maggie, that's one less flower in the pot."

I would have protested, but the cider swirled around my head and now soured my stomach. I belched like I was back in the pie-and-mash shop. My face flushed. "Rather a heavy lunch."

Uncle grinned. "Now, Boots, call up to the house. Her Ladyship is expecting Miss Darling. I shall remain here with you"—he winked at Boots—"in the relative safety of the carriage house."

"Aye, that is a wise decision." Boots turned to look at me. "I hear Her Ladyship is in one of her... well, she's a little like a mother hen, if you know what I mean."

"Pecking everything in sight," added Uncle Tristan.

Boots nodded. "Aye, that would be about right." He pointed to a large metal contraption. "And now Sir Sandoe 'as bought an envelope rack that Lady Herriman leaves me notes in to run about and deliver. You'd think I was the postman." With a grunt, he disappeared into the carriage house.

Moments later, a tall, dapper man, with a hairline moustache and an army haircut, strode towards us. If it were not for the white gloves and uniform, which seemed to comprise almost entirely of highly polished brass buttons, I would have taken him for the lord of the manor.

"That's Tom Withers, the head butler—devil of a temper," whispered Uncle Tristan. "The man runs this place with the harsh whip of a circus ringmaster. Here, take these papers, and remember to eat humble pie with Her Ladyship."

"Anything else?"

"Don't get too close; try to stick to the dark corners."

Uncle Tristan turned, and with a slight sway, strode towards the carriage house.

"Miss Darling?" Withers bowed as he spoke, but his sharp eyes never left my face.

"Indeed," I said, hoping he couldn't smell the alcohol on my breath.

His nose twitched. "I'm Withers, the head butler. Lady Herriman will see you shortly." He hesitated then said, "You are the young niece of Mr Tristan Harbottle?"

"That's me." I smiled but already felt Uncle's plan was unravelling.

"From London?"

"Yes."

"To help with his staffing business?"

"That is so."

Withers pointed his nose to the sky and sniffed. "I shall have to speak with the outside lads about the consumption of alcohol during work hours. It is rather unbecoming, don't you think?"

I swayed, let lose another belch, and mumbled, "Indeed it is."

Chapter 15

"THIS WAY, MADAM."

Withers made a sharp turn and strode away. I followed him along a gravel path that ran alongside the main house. We turned left at the end onto a narrow dirt trail.

I said, "Is this the way to the servants' quarters?"

"Yes, madam. Today, we shall use the tradesmen's entrance, as this is a business, rather than a social visit."

We walked for several minutes, and I wondered just how much farther when Withers stopped, reached out a hand, and pulled on a latch which I'd have missed. A door swung open, and we entered a dim hallway.

White tiles lined the floor. A faded, dingy, grey paint covered the walls. The smell of food cooking mingled with the sharp clank of metallic pots and mumbled voices from unseen rooms.

As we continued to walk, I realised I knew little about Lady Herriman. I wanted to discover more about the woman ahead of our meeting. Withers would know everything. But how to get him to talk?

When I worked in the pie-and-mash shop, a friendly smile and simple questions often opened a floodgate. I used that knowledge now to open tight-lipped Withers.

"Wonderful weather we are having."

"Yes, madam."

"Did you see the union protestors?"

"Certainly, madam."

"How many staff do you employ here, Withers?"

"I couldn't say, madam."

"How long have you been here?"

"One doesn't like to count the years, madam."

My attempts crashed on the barren rocks of his curt responses. I tried again.

"Do you like it here?"

"To serve is my only purpose in life, madam."

I was getting nowhere, so I went for the direct question. "What is Her Ladyship like?"

Withers stopped, turned, gave me a withering look, and said, "Lady Herriman is a lady, madam."

I gave up after that and followed him meekly along the hallway and up a narrow staircase, at the end of which we turned right into a scullery.

It was a small room with large windows which looked out onto a small yard surrounded by a brick wall. There was a row of bells above a large iron sink, shelves filled with glass bottles and clay jars. Several flat irons hung on wall brackets. Three ironing boards leaned against another wall. To one side was a wooden kitchen table, with a half-eaten crust of bread, cheese, and the remains of a meat pie. On another long, low table rested a pile of freshly ironed, starched linens. Underneath, I saw a small black-and-white kitten. It watched us enter and scratched. The poor thing only had three legs.

Withers stopped, and his body visibly stiffened. For a moment, he seemed to forget my presence, and I watched with fascination as his eyes turned black, lower lip purpled, and thick blue veins bulged at the sides of his neck. Then he spoke, his voice a cold whisper. "What is the meaning of this wasted food?"

There was no answer from the empty room.

Withers stomped to the kitchen table, swiped the plate and its contents onto the floor. As the clatter echoed around the scullery, an older woman came hurrying. Behind her was a young girl, no older than twelve, with her eyes wide open.

The older woman said, "Sorry, Master Withers, we was just 'avin a break. Me niece, young Rose, is new, and she needed a—"

"To the devil with your excuses, Mrs Mullins, and to the devil with your niece Rose."

Mrs Mullins placed her hands on her hips. "Now, Master Withers, I—"

"Shut up, you hag!"

Withers strode over to the linen table. His shoulders trembled with barely concealed rage. The shudder rolled along his back. When it reached his legs, he raised his right foot and kicked the table with brute force. It toppled over, scattering the clothes on the floor.

The kitten screeched.

Withers swung a foot at the poor, unfortunate creature, missed, and in a blind fury stomped and kicked the linens with his polished shoes.

When the anger subsided, he ran a finger over his hairline moustache and said, "This lot needs rewashing, starching, and ironing. And that cat needs poisoning."

Mrs Mullins, face red, wiped her hands on her apron. "Withers, you oaf! Little Rose stood 'ere all day sorting, sprinkling, folding, and ironing that lot. And Swiftee is only a kitten; he ain't done no wrong."

"Shall I see to it, Mrs Mullins," began Withers in a soft voice, "that today is your last?"

"But I'm a widow; this job is all I've got." Mrs Mullins lowered her head. "Sorry, sir, I spoke out of turn. Rose, gather up those linens and get to rewashing 'em."

Rose's teeth chattered; her eyes had dark ugly lines under them. She shambled, stooped, and gathered up the items. Then she turned to Withers, her eyes wide and pleading. "But Swiftee is a lovely kitten. We play together. Can we let him be, please?"

"Rose," snarled Withers, "you are to see to it that blasted cat gets a good dose of rat poison. Leave the filthy beast's body outside of my quarters. And don't you go running to Sir Sandoe with complaints. He has given me a free hand with you servants. What I say is the law. Now, both of you, go!"

Mrs Mullins and Rose left. Withers turned, and half jumped when he saw me. In an instant, the purple colour drained from his face. A moment later, his back straightened, and he'd regained his composure.

With a dignified white-gloved hand, he reached out and tugged a long cord that hung from the ceiling. I thought I heard the tinkle of a distant bell, although that might have been my imagination, the cider, or both.

Withers pulled a silver pendant from his jacket pocket, let it swing back and forth for a moment. "Memories are just a jumble of recollections. And you recall nothing at all."

"Pardon?"

"Beautiful, isn't it. Watch the pendant."

"No!" I snapped. "Have you lost your mind?"

He jerked the pendent into his pocket, stared full into my eyes with barely concealed fury, and said, "Miss Darling, I'm sure in London you've seen your fair share of petty thievery. We've experienced it here. A wooden display case of five irreplaceable Victorian hunting knives went missing a few years back. Her Ladyship was most displeased."

Annoyed at the man's shenanigans and the implication of his words, I said, "And what has that to do with me?"

Withers' lips curved into a smirk. "One can never be too careful who one invites into a great house like this. I shall wait with you until Miss Trimmings appears. She is a trusted and reliable member of staff."

Chapter 16

I'D EXPECTED A SMALL scrawny woman in a black maid's dress, a white half apron of ruffled lace, and a matching headpiece.

Dolly Trimmings wore none of that. A silver star pattern shimmered on her black silk gown. Gold bracelets jangled around her wrists, and a string of pearls hung about her thick neck.

Miss Trimmings took my hands in her plump grip. She was a large overweight woman about my age, with eyes that twitched like a bird and the wide mouth of a hippopotamus. And she was panting like a greyhound.

"Is that you, Miss Darling? Oh Gawd, yes, yes, it is you!"

She threw her arms about me. The woman had the grip of a bear. There was a strong whiff of plum wine about her person.

When we separated, Miss Trimmings glanced me up and down. "Ain't be waiting long, 'ave ya?"

I was still trying to make sense of her warm welcome. It was as if we were old friends, but I've never before set eyes on the woman.

"Oh, no, not long at all," I said, watching Withers leave. "We just arrived."

"Good, let us sit at the table for a short moment while I catches me breath. Rooms in Bagington Hall always 'ave two stairways. Those for the ladies and gentlemen and those for the servants." Dolly took in a large gulp of air. "My, look at all that linen. Mrs Mullins is behind today."

We sat at the kitchen table where Miss Trimmings said, "Ain't you wondering how I knew it was you, seeing as we 'ave never met afore just now?"

I said, "That thought had crossed my mind, Miss Trimmings."

"Please, everyone calls me Dolly, even Her Ladyship."

"Dolly, how did you know it was I?"

Her thick lips curved upward. "I've the knack, you see. I can identify people by the curl of their lip and angle of the eye. Few can do that, but ole Dolly can. Your face is like a fingerprint: unique. I remembers the details and never forgets 'em."

"Ah! That is interesting." Dolly's skill was rather an odd one, and I wondered how it aided her as a chambermaid. "Does it help you identify guests?"

"And members of the same family." Dolly peered into my face and chuckled. "You are most certainly the niece of Mr Harbottle." After a moment, she said, "He said you were seventeen!"

Panic shot through my body; the game was up.

Oh bother!

For some seconds, I could neither think nor speak but stood there paralysed. Then words bubbled into my mind, formed into a coherent sentence, and came out in a light, jovial tone.

"Ha-ha, yes. I was much younger seventeen years ago when I last met Uncle Tristan."

Dolly said, "Mr Harbottle enjoys his little games, don't he? On that account, I'm still twenty-one!"

We both laughed. Dolly with genuine mirth. And I with genuine relief.

Standing at the shop counter in a pie-and-mash shop, you meet all sorts, and Dolly was the instant-friend type, the class of person who never met a stranger. And I have found in serving hundreds of customers, that type of person also likes to talk.

I said, "Dolly, tell me about Sir Sandoe."

A light lit in her birdlike eyes. "What is it you want to know?"

"Does he have children?"

"His wife died a while back, and he only has a single child: a daughter, Antoinette."

I thought for a moment then said, "I suppose I shall see her?"

"Oh, no, miss. You shan't see her."

"Why not?"

"I can't say."

I placed my hands on the table. "Is it because Antoinette is ill... in the mind?"

Dolly laughed. "Miss Darling, the next thing you'll be telling me is that Sir Sandoe put pretty Antoinette away in Sharrington Insane Asylum."

"I heard something to that effect."

"Well, it ain't true. Sharrington Asylum only took men, and anyway, it closed down years ago. No, Sir Sandoe didn't put gorgeous Antoinette away."

"Then what happened to her?"

Dolly sat very still, her head tilted towards the door as if listening for something. After a moment, she said, "Can't be too careful what you say around here; the walls 'ave ears."

She needed a little encouragement, so I said, "Dolly, I shan't say a word."

Dolly placed her fat hand on her pearl necklace and said, "Antoinette got mixed up with Lady Blackwood and her group fighting for social justice."

"Pardon?"

"Politicking for women's rights. I suppose the final straw came when Antoinette got involved in the agricultural union."

I said, "To fight for fair pay?"

"And so women could join." Dolly lowered her voice. "Antoinette ran off three years ago with a union organiser. The last I heard, the couple set sail for America and ain't never been seen since. Sir Sandoe spread the rumour about Sharrington Asylum to spare embarrassment."

Everything became clear with her words. Antoinette was in America with her sweetheart, and Sir Sandoe made up a cock-and-bull story to save face. A sense of relief washed over me. In America, Antoinette would be safe, and I felt certain she would continue her fight for women's rights.

Now I wondered about Dolly's fine clothes and jewellery. I said, "Lovely pearls, where did you buy them?"

"Oh, no, I couldn't afford these on my pay! Neither this dress." She let out a little self-conscious laugh. "They belong to Lady Herriman. I likes to 'borrow' her cast-offs when she ain't looking."

I tried to hide the look of shock on my face. "You are wearing Lady Herriman's wardrobe?"

Dolly winked and said, "Our little secret, eh?"

I wasn't sure what to say. The woman was sharing things with me as if we were childhood friends. What was I to think? I said, "Now, listen, I'm not sure you should—"

Dolly raised a hand, her thick lips twisted into a smile. "I borrowed a silk scarf for your uncle—bright orange. Anyway, I always return everything. Now there ain't no harm in that, is there? I've worked for Her Ladyship over ten years. It's a perk of the job."

The mention of Lady Herriman reminded me of the upcoming meeting. I said, "Dolly, is Her Ladyship in good spirits this afternoon?"

"Like a bear woken from hibernation in deep winter. Ain't never seen her in such a foul mood."

That didn't sound good. "Perhaps I should call at another time."

"Her Ladyship is a stickler with appointments."

"But her foul mood?"

"That's on my account." Again, Dolly winked. "Lady Herriman can't find her lorgnette spectacles. When I introduce you, try to stay in the shadows."

"Ah, I see!"

"I'll 'ave the devil to pay, I suppose." Dolly twiddled with her pearls and grinned. "But it don't matter, cos soon I'll be a lady too."

"Really?"

Dolly gazed over her shoulder then lowered her voice. "Before this year is out, I'm gonna be a wealthy woman, just like Her Ladyship."

"An inheritance?"

Dolly said, "Don't 'ave no money in my family; we are all dirt poor." She placed a finger to her lip. "Sir Sandoe put aside my pay these past five years to buy shares in a gold mine in Peru. News of a discovery is due before the year is out."

Chapter 17

DOLLY ENTERED LADY Herriman's dim antechamber on tiptoe.

I followed close behind.

"Miss Darling for you, madam," said Dolly as she gave a little bow and withdrew, walking backwards, her back stooped.

I stood stock-still while my eyes adjusted to the gloom. A chink of light illuminated the outline of the heavy curtains that draped a large window. To one side, in a terracotta pot, a tired aspidistra stretched towards the light. The edges of furniture came slowly into view: a mahogany table, a Victorian writing desk, a Georgian side cabinet facing the window, a gilt-legged console table against a wall above which hung a tall mirror. Upon the mantelpiece, a marble clock jostled for space with bronzes of horses and a pair of wrought-iron candlesticks.

Then I saw them, and for a moment, I stood in bewilderment. In the centre of the room, in a large glass case, a lion, with a fanged mouth opened wide, stared back. In another case, a tiger with vicious claws, and in yet another, a leopard in full stride. Beyond the cases, I saw several portraits of an attractive, young woman dressed in full hunting gear.

"Do you hunt, Miss Darling?"

The question came from the far side of the room. I turned towards the voice. The outline of a figure took shape. My mouth opened and closed, throat suddenly dry. Whatever I had expected of Lady Herriman, it was not this.

She stood in a dark corner with an oversized goblet in her left hand and a giant black Bible tucked under her right arm. I hadn't inquired about her age, but she looked older than Mr Gunthorpe, and he died at ninety-eight.

She wore an outfit that might have once bedecked the wardrobe of Queen Victoria. Grotesque, black marks traced out her eyebrows; her face was stiff with pale powder; irregular, red splotches adorned her hollow cheeks, and red lip rouge was plastered about her thin lips, which were drawn back into an unpleasant smile revealing two crooked rows of rotted teeth.

On top of her head stood an exuberant Elizabethan wig, resplendent with giant white coils that rose like the peaks in a mountain range.

"No... I... well... there isn't much call for it in London." I tried not to stare but couldn't take my eyes off those eyebrows, the massive wig, the sunken cheeks. In fact, I couldn't take my eyes off the entire woman.

Lady Herriman sighed. "I suppose not. I learned to shoot in Kenya, got a taste for it. Alas, the little red foxes we have about Norfolk do not offer the same satisfaction as the African lion or Indian tiger." As she spoke, her thin lips seemed to take over her entire face. "Are you the niece of Mr Harbottle?"

I took a leaf from Withers' book and kept my answers short. "Yes, madam. That is correct." I threw in a curtsy for good measure.

Her eyes pierced through the gloom. "Mr Harbottle's young niece, down from London?"

I didn't like the direction of the conversation, but it was too late to back out now. I bowed. "That is correct, Lady Herriman."

Lady Herriman said, "Oh, my child, I am so sorry for you. I've just come from my private chapel where I offered a special prayer for your uncle."

I hoped it involved gold mines in Peru but said, "Thank you, Lady Herriman."

"Dear child, I have an illness that admits no cure. That is why my rooms must remain darkened. But I do not pray for my own sufferings. That I bear without complaint."

"Most courageous, Lady Herriman." I was getting the hang of the Withers' short-answer thing.

"Miss Darling, it says in the good book, 'Do nothing from rivalry or conceit, but in humility count others more significant than yourselves.' I believe this is a message for your uncle."

I said, "How so, Lady Herriman?"

"Mr Harbottle is so puffed up with conceit, I fear he might burst. The last time we met, he wore a repulsive orange scarf about his neck. Why, have you ever seen such a vile parade of colour on a man?"

There was nothing I could say to that, so I remained silent, eyes cast down in deference.

"And the man wilfully disobeyed orders." Lady Herriman took another sip from the goblet and swayed a little. "I said to your uncle, the very first thing I would like him to do is throw out all the servants, except Dolly and Withers. I need young blood about me, not a bunch of stodgy old-timers."

I opened my mouth to say something but decided it was best to keep it shut.

Lady Herriman continued, "Boots needs starving for a week, and as for Vicar Humberstone—"

For a moment, I forgot myself and said, "But Boots is already too thin, and as for the vicar,is he a member of your staff?" Then I added quickly, "Madam."

"If it were down to me, I'd have the man horsewhipped. For a rural man of the cloth, he spends entirely too much time mingling with common people. It is little wonder the church is in decline. Withers is the only decent individual on the entire staff. That man never raises his voice and often joins me in prayers for the unfortunate and poor. Oh, it is so trying to be surrounded by a bunch of Norfolk halfwits. That is why you intrigue me so, Miss Darling. London staff are sophisticated. They understand their role in life is to serve their superiors."

The woman's outlook was even more dated than Sir Sandoe. I wanted to drop off the papers and get away from Lady Herriman before the cider made me say something I'd later regret. I sucked in a breath but sensed there was more and kept my mouth shut.

"My in-law, Sir Sandoe, insists we keep the current staff. And your uncle agrees with him." Lady Herriman batted at a stray curl on her wig. "This is the nineteen twenties where all the talk is of universal suffrage, yet he keeps me confined to this place like a lunatic in a sanatorium: no hunting, no high-society balls, and scarcely a visitor. Bagington Hall has become my tomb, but I am not dead yet!"

Lady Herriman drained her goblet, stepped forward, and craned her neck like an ancient ostrich. Even at a distance and through the gloom, I could sense her eyes roving over my face.

"Goodness, how the young are aged these days. Have you tried an overnight coat of opium, followed by an ammonia wash the following morning? It does wonders for the pallor."

"Thank you. Yes, I shall make a note of it." But soap and water were the extent of my daily face-cleansing routine, and I was content with the results.

Lady Herriman said, "Miss Darling, how did you find London?"

"Very busy, and foggy during the winter months."

"Ah, yes. That was so in my day." Lady Herriman turned towards the tall mirror, tidied a stray curl, and studied herself in the glass. She raised her chin, pursed her lips, and lowered her eyelids. With a satisfied grunt, she took a sip from her goblet and turned back. "Miss Darling, how old am I?"

"I wouldn't like to say."

"Guess."

This was a dangerous game. One I didn't want to play. "My uncle has asked I deliver these papers for your review."

"Ah, yes. Alas, I do not have my lorgnette spectacles; Dolly has misplaced them. I shall review the papers later and get word to your uncle of my satisfaction. Now, as to my age, you didn't answer my question." Lady Herriman turned back to the mirror, lifted a wasted hand, and delicately touched her white wig with the tips of thin, bejewelled fingers. "My age, Miss Darling, what would you guess?"

In a panic, I said the first thing that came to my head. "Forty-two."

Again, the thin red lips took over her face, this time curling up into a smile. "Really, well, that is so gratifying. I'd have put you about the same age. You are dismissed."

Chapter 18

"HER LADYSHIP WAS SMILING; that is unusual," said Dolly as we walked down a flight of stairs. "What did you say to her?"

I shrugged. "Not sure, but I'm glad the audience is over."

At the bottom of the stairs, we made a sharp turn, walked a few feet then made another turn. The door to the scullery came into view.

Inside, Dolly said, "Here we are. Take a seat at the kitchen table. Withers will be 'ere in a moment to walk you back to the carriage house. I've got to get back to 'ave a little rest and me afternoon tipple of plum wine. It was nice meeting you, Miss Darling."

Alone at the kitchen table, I thought about Lady Herriman. She differed from what I'd expected. The word unusual didn't do her justice. And what about Dolly? She didn't fit my expectations of a chambermaid either.

"An odd pair."

But strangely, they seemed to fit together, almost like a hand fits into a glove. That made me think of Withers. The man moved about as if he were the lord of the manor and had a fiery temper to match. I knew now there was also a streak of meanness hidden just under his surface. I shuddered, grateful that I didn't have to work for him. Where was he?

I glanced around the empty scullery. Not much to see. Two doors, the one I entered with Dolly was closed. The other entry, used by Mrs Mullins and her niece, was half-open. There was the wooden linen table, flat irons on the wall, ironing boards, the row of bells above the sink, a small empty bowl for the kitten.

Footsteps sounded along a hallway.

"Ah, Miss Darling, I take it your audience with Lady Herriman has concluded?" Withers peered around the room as if assessing all was in order. "Let us return to the carriage house."

Meow, meow, meow.

Swiftee hobbled into the kitchen. I wanted to pick the little thing up but remembered my allergic reaction to cats and sneezed.

Withers glared. "What the dickens!"

Swiftee scampered under the linen table where he sat with his body bunched up and his head thrust forward watching us.

Meow, meow, meow.

"Revolting, deformed devil of a creature. I'll do you in myself, right now!" Withers' lower lip purpled, thick blue veins bulged at the sides of his neck. From a pocket, he pulled out a small knife and a length of string curved in the shape of a noose. "Here, kitty."

I felt a cold chill of horror. "Withers, I'll take the kitten home with me."

Withers spun around; his lower lip trembled. "Madam, that ugly beast won't be any good as a rat catcher, not with three legs. Best let me see to him now. It will only take a moment."

"That's all right, Withers. I'll keep him as a house cat." The words came from my heart, but my head wondered how I'd make it out of Bagington Hall without collapsing in a fit of sneezes. I could already feel my throat closing, and that was at the thought of it. But I refused to let the kitten suffer.

Withers placed a finger on his hairline moustache and for a moment did not move; then with a sharp jerk of his head, he said, "Fine, madam. Take it with you."

Ding, ding, ding...

A bell above the sink swung back and forth.

Withers muttered something under his breath. "That'll be Lady Herriman. I shall return in a moment. Then I shall escort you and the kitten off the premises. Please stay here."

When he was gone, I stooped on all fours.

"Here, Swiftee, come to Maggie."

The kitten stepped towards me.

I sneezed.

Swiftee stopped then turned and limped towards the open door.

"Swiftee!"

He hobbled from the scullery.

Quickly, I got to my feet. I hesitated for long enough to decide. If I didn't get Swiftee before Withers returned, he was done for.

I sneezed and set off at little more than a trot, all the while hoping the wee creature hadn't gone too far.

"Swiftee, come back. Your life depends on it."

Chapter 19

I FOLLOWED SWIFTEE into a shabby, grey hallway. It stretched ahead for about twenty feet then hit a corner. Paint peeled off the wall, and there was the heavy odour of mildew.

"Swiftee."

Withers would be back at any moment. Time was running out for my rescue. But there was no sign of the tiny animal.

"Here, Swiftee."

How in the world did a three-legged kitten disappear so quickly? I paced a few steps along the corridor and stopped.

"No, he couldn't have gone this way."

I turned back towards the scullery. The door was ajar. Had the kitten doubled back into the room?

"Yes, that's the only possibility."

I retraced my steps.

As I approached the scullery entrance, I saw a movement out of the corner of my eye.

Meow, meow.

I looked down.

Swiftee sat in a recess in the wall, his eyes wide and unblinking. The indentation, a handbreadth deep, stretched from the floor to the ceiling and was about three feet wide. Only now, as my eyes adjusted fully to the gloom, did I make out the outline of a door.

As I stood there blinking, I realised the entire door was painted over in the grey colour of the corridor. This included the small metallic doorknob and the wood around the doorpost. I guessed it was a sealed doorway to an unused part of Bagington Hall.

"Crafty little kitty."

I stooped down to pick up Swiftee.

He vanished as my hand closed about him.

Startled, I straightened up. "What on earth!"

It wasn't until I stared hard at the space that I saw a small irregular hole in the bottom wooden panel where the thick wood had rotted away. Swiftee was on the other side of the door.

Quickly, I glanced at the door handle then both ways along the corridor. I gave it a tug. It shifted a fraction. I tugged harder and pulled, with a grunt. It was solid and heavy. Again, I pulled. The door screeched open, shuddering and groaning as if in protest.

A waft of putrid, warm air rushed out. A narrow staircase went up at a steep angle. At the top, I could make out the dim glow of daylight. Swiftee sat on the fifth step.

"Come here, Swiftee."

He regarded me with curiosity but didn't move.

With care, I edged towards him. The first step, the second step, the third step.

Swiftee didn't move.

With one arm balanced against the rough brick wall, I stepped onto the fourth step, stooped down, and picked him up. To his credit, the kitten didn't protest.

Thud.

All went dark.

For a brief, dreadful second I stood there in the pitch black, dazed and confused. Then I cried, "The door!"

But my cries were fruitless. It had swung shut!

The sunlight shining from the top of the stairs was enough for me to see. With Swiftee under my right arm, I edged towards the door, sneezed, tugged the handle, and pushed.

Crack.

To my horror, the handle came off in my hand.

"Oh bother!"

My throat went dry and began to contract, and I knew it wasn't only due to Swiftee. The solid door was shut tight—I was trapped.

With my left hand, I felt around for the steel pin. If I could twist it, the door would open. But I'm not left handed, so I fumbled and pushed the pin farther away.

"I should have used my right hand!"

I turned, placed Swiftee on the step, and returned to the door.

The kitten scampered up the stairs.

"Swiftee, come back!"

I stood there, paralysed with indecision. Follow the kitten or get out of here?

I turned back to the door. I had to get it open, then I'd get the kitten.

Anxiously, I poked around for the steel pin. After several feverish moments, there was a sharp metallic thud in the corridor. The handle on the other side had fallen off.

"Oh bother, bother, bother! This is your fault, Swiftee."

A cold sweat broke out on my forehead. I felt as if I'd entered a tomb. My tomb.

Visions of my desiccated corpse with a kitten in my arms flashed through my mind. Now I was dangerously close to panic but knew I must control my thinking if I wanted to get out quickly.

What was the worst thing that could happen?

I thought of the unidentified sounds familiar to old houses, of spectres floating down the staircase, and of giant rats with sharp fangs for teeth. All these thoughts swirled around like a dry wind whipping up ashes into a blazing fire of dread.

"Don't be silly, Maggie," I said, trying to get a grip on my fears. "After all, the biggest rat you've ever seen was in London—Mr Pritchard!"

That made me laugh. There was nothing to worry about. Uncle Tristan would come looking for me as would Withers. But a doubt came creeping slowly into my mind. Why would Uncle Tristan or Withers look here? After all, I'd barely noticed the entrance myself.

"I have to open that door and get out of here with Swiftee."

Now, with panic brewing, I tried to feel around the doorpost for a crack large enough to get some leverage. When that didn't work, I pounded on the heavy door, yelled, and kicked the wood.

But no one came running.

On the edge of blind panic, I threw my weight against the solid wood, then again and again.

The door held.

I shouted, hating the fear in my voice, hating myself for being angry with a little kitten—a three-legged waif whose life lay in my hands.

Fatigued, I slumped against the solid wood. As I gasped in the rotten air, Dolly Trimmings' remarks flitted into my mind. "Rooms in Bagington Hall always 'ave two stairways. Those for the ladies and gentlemen and those for the servants."

With my mind oddly clarified by the apple cider, I climbed the stairs into the dim glow of daylight.

Chapter 20

THIS CAN'T BE RIGHT. Swiftee and his curiosity. Oh bother!

I stared in bewildered disbelief. I'd hoped the stairs led to a large room with floor-to-ceiling glass windows overlooking a beautiful part of the grounds of Bagington Hall.

Or perhaps a smaller place, bedecked in regal furniture with a soft carpet and heavily patterned wallpaper, abundantly decorated with the sweeping curves of exotic birds or vegetation. After all, it was clearly a servants' staircase, and hadn't Dolly said there were separate stairs for the ladies and gentlemen?

But the space was tiny, with tall brick walls on all four sides and a large skylight from which a blazing sun shone illuminating rays. Instantly, it reminded me of Uncle Tristan's office—a storage loft, but a miniature version and without the stench of curing hides.

I stepped into the room. The rough wooden floorboards shuddered and squeaked. It was like walking into the past. There was an old escritoire used long ago as a writing desk. A small dust-ridden oak case rested with its glass lid open, the contents long gone. There was a lopsided Louis Quinze settee, a tall gold-rimmed mirror clouded with age, a dried-up washstand, and other relics of a bygone era.

And in the middle of the room was a great iron bed, piled with dust-ridden sheets.

Everything was old or decrepit or useless, even the writing desk. For several moments, I stared at the dusty item. It was tall, like a mini wardrobe, made of oak and mahogany. I'd seen scores of them at auction in London, but because of their size and bulk they had fallen from favour.

I suppose it was the writing surface that caught my attention. It was extended out as if its last user was in the middle of composing a letter. But the inkwell had long since dried up, the paper turned to dust. Maybe it once belonged to Lady Herriman or perhaps her father?

The groan of the floorboards interrupted my thoughts. I glanced down at the bare wooden slats and exposed nails. Were they even sound?

With care, I took another step towards the iron bed. It was ancient: brown, chipped paint with gold, Victorian swirls on both the footrest and headrest. How long since it was last used?

I tilted my head back to gaze up through the skylight, half expecting to see something other than blue. But the sky was all there was to see.

"Swiftee!"

Something scurried by my feet. I spun around and looked down.

Swiftee crouched low at the footrest, stone still as if watching a mouse. I stooped down to pick him up. He scampered into my arms without a fuss.

"I think we must leave the same way we got in," I mumbled. "Through that big, ugly wooden door. Are you with me?"

And then it happened. The sun dipped behind a cloud casting the room into a gloomy haze. The room went cold. A voice called out.

"Hello!"

I jumped, staggered back, falling onto the bed. A plume of dust darkened the room. Swiftee wriggled free from my arms. As I tugged on the sheets to stand up, I couldn't believe what I saw peeping out from the top of the bed.

For several seconds, I gaped with more surprise than when I watched George Edwards eating a cobnut on the train to Cromer. Then I struggled to my feet, found my knees too weak to support me, and fell back onto the bed.

Another plume of dust filled the air.

I rolled to the hard floor, felt my stomach lurch, and clapped my hands to my mouth as cold seeped through my bones. Because what I saw was the blackened head of a woman.

Chapter 21

FRANTIC, I STRUGGLED to my knees.

Again, came the voice. "Hello!"

In my terrified state, the words seemed to drift up from the bed. But that couldn't be!

More words echoed around the room. "Good heavens."

I twisted towards the door.

"Hello! Good heavens." It was Mrs Mullins, her face flushed with the effort of climbing the stairs. "I heard a pounding from the corridor and had a devil of a job opening the door. This is the old chambermaid's quarters, not used in years. What are you doing in here?"

On my trembling feet, I pointed with a quivering hand to the bed.

Mrs Mullins' eyes widened. She tipped her head back and let loose a shriek more terrifying than my discovery.

Then she fainted.

Within five minutes, household staff filled the room. It was standing room only as eager eyes and fingers pointed at the desiccated body on the bed. Word soon spread to the ground staff. Boots was the first to arrive, his long swan-like neck at full stretch, eyes enormous. Not until Withers came did a semblance of order take hold.

"Everyone out, except Miss Darling and Mrs Mullins," Withers boomed.

But the crowd were too excited to take much notice at first.

"I'll see to it that today is your last day at Bagington Hall," he screeched.

There was a general murmur of discontent which grew loudest from those waiting their turn near the bottom of the steps. It seemed everyone wanted to see the gruesome exhibit.

Withers let loose his ferocious temper. "Be off with you. Get out!"

Eventually, grudgingly, they drifted away.

"Out, now!" boomed Withers at Boots who lingered as if savouring the last drop of a fine wine.

"Aye, sir. Thought I wanted to work inside where it is all comfortable on a cold winter's day. Right next to the fire, that's what I dreamed of. But no thank you. I prefers the chill winds of me carriage house."

By this time, Mrs Mullins had revived, a kind household member having brought a large bottle of plum wine and a glass to calm her nerves. The bottle lay half empty. "Master Withers," she slurred. "I knows who it is. I knows whose body is a lying there on that bed all blacked and dried like a summer prune."

"The police will be here in a short while," replied Withers. "We will have none of your rumour or speculation."

"But I knows," protested Mrs Mullins, emboldened by the plum wine, "ain't you or anyone else going to keep me quiet."

Withers glared at the woman. "Shut up, you hag!"

I suspected he was more furious at her defiance than anything else. I said, "Please tell us what you know, Mrs Mullins."

Withers turned his glare on me. "Sir Sandoe will hear of this whole incident shortly. We don't want to spread any silly rumours until the police have had a chance to look over the facts, do we?"

Mrs Mullins muttered, "It don't matter. It don't matter. We'll be seeking work when the truth is told. All that glitters ain't gold."

I said, "Speak up, woman. Don't let the pompous fool bully you. Who is it?"

But Mrs Mullins didn't have to say a word. Dolly Trimmings hurried into the room. "Lady Herriman sent me to investigate the fuss," she said, standing at the door, wide eyes fixed on the blackened head. After a moment, her voice dropped to a whisper. "Cor blimey, Withers, it is Miss Antoinette! I thought she'd run off to America with that union fellow."

Chapter 22

"GO ON, 'AVE ANOTHER cup of tea, and put plenty of sugar in it," urged Dolly.

"Don't mind if I do cos my bloody feet are killing me," replied Sergeant Pender. He was a tall broad-shouldered man with a narrow face. His eyes were sunk deep into his head as if they'd seen too much and were frightened to see any more. "Nothing like a nice cuppa on a day like this eases the nerves."

Dolly, Mrs Mullins, and I were sitting around the kitchen table in the scullery each having given a brief statement to the sergeant. Swiftee sat firmly in my lap. We were waiting for the return of Chief Inspector Little, who went with Withers to speak with Lady Herriman.

"It must 'ave been a terrible shock to you," said Dolly, her thick lips curved slightly at the edges as if holding back a secret. "I mean, don't suppose you're called out to a big 'ouse on account of a body every day."

Sergeant Pender's slender head moved in affirmation. "Aye, but it happens more than you'd like to think about, but they don't pay me enough to go about investigating. I leave all that to the chief inspector. I'm just a regular walk-the-beat type of police officer, and that's the way I like it." He took a long slow gulp of tea, his eyelids drooping. "But, yes, it was a shock to the system, as I came over 'ere on account of a telephone call from the gatekeeper."

Dolly said, "About the body of poor dear Miss Antoinette?"

The sergeant shook his head. "The agricultural strike. This business with the union is causing a cartload of trouble. Not that I can blame 'em for putting down tools. Can't say I'd readily agree to work longer hours for less pay either."

Mrs Mullins said, "The household workers ought to form a union and strike too! Pay and conditions is terrible 'ere, but what choice do we 'ave?"

Dolly's lips became a straight line. "Now, listen here, Mrs Mullins. Lady Herriman and Sir Sandoe have been good to keep us on."

"It's all right for them that gets to drink their plum wine from goblets and wear fancy pearls they don't own," said Mrs Mullins, her voice a high-pitched bark.

Sergeant Pender raised a hand to quell the argument. "Let's not be politicking today; that's for them in parliament. Now where was I?"

"Talking about why you came over to Bagington Hall in the first place," said Dolly.

The sergeant said, "We got a call about a disturbance at the gatehouse. A young fellow by the name of Frank Perry, bold as a lion, with a desperate look. Not from around these parts either, said he wanted to speak with Sir Sandoe."

"Why?" Dolly, Mrs Mullins, and I said together.

"The young man said he had a letter that would interest Sir Sandoe."

Mrs Mullins opened her mouth to speak. Dolly flashed her a hard glare and in a slow movement placed a finger to her lips. The two women sat quietly for a moment watching each other. Our cups of tea sat before us on the table, steam rising in great swirls.

After thirty seconds of silence, Mrs Mullins' lips twitched. She picked up her cup and took a hesitant sip then said, "You were saying, Sergeant?"

Sergeant Pender's slender face seemed to constrict slightly and draw tight about his cheeks. But he continued as if unaware of what had taken place between the two women. "Mr Perry wouldn't give me the letter—"

Dolly interrupted. "What reason could this Frank Perry 'ave for wanting to give a letter to Sir Sandoe? The whole thing is ridiculous."

"So I searched his pockets. They were empty as I expected, save a knife. Old looking, long handle, a hunting knife." Sergeant Pender let out a satisfied chuckle. "Let me tell you, I gave the young fellow a stern talking to and sent him on his way."

Now Sergeant Pender turned to Mrs Mullins, and once again, his narrow face seemed to constrict. "There was something you were going to say. Let's be having ya; spit it out, woman."

Mrs Mullins looked down, her rough fingers toying with her cup. "It was just—"

"Slice of seed cake, Sergeant?" Dolly got to her feet. "I'm sure we 'ave some around here, don't we, Mrs Mullins?"

The sergeant became very still, and I thought I saw a flash of indecision in his eyes.

"Let's leave the investigating to them that gets paid for it," said Dolly in a soft voice. "Now, Sergeant, how about a nice drop of plum wine to go with that seed cake?"

Sergeant Pender's face relaxed. "Aye, I wouldn't say no." He lolled back in his seat, eased his feet onto a vacant chair, eyes half closing. "Pour it in a mug, so it doesn't look like I'm drinking on duty when the chief inspector returns."

Chapter 23

WITHERS ANNOUNCED CHIEF Inspector Little with a low bow. As he did so, he turned his head towards Dolly. If I hadn't been paying attention, what happened next would have gone undetected.

No words passed from the lips of Withers, but there was a slight lowering of the eyelids, an almost indiscernible downwards curve at the edge of his lips and a flicker of frown lines across his forehead.

In return, Dolly raised her chin a fraction of a degree. She placed a chubby hand on her cheek like a scientist pondering the answer to one of nature's mysteries. With a smooth movement, her head dipped then rose.

The chambermaid and the butler were definitely in communication about something but about what was beyond me.

Chief Inspector Little strode into the scullery. He wore a drab brown suit with a black bowler hat atop an undersized head and walked with a military-style goose-step. His black boots clattered against the tile floor with an authoritative thwack.

"An absolutely beastly discovery, Sergeant Pender," Chief Inspector Little said, stopping by the table. His small face, plum nose, angular bristled eyebrows, and unblinking eyes gave him the look of a startled squirrel.

"Bloody awful, sir."

The chief inspector nodded. "I'd go up there to poke around a little myself if it weren't for the odd touch of lumbago. Picked it up during the war." He peered down at the table. "A hot mug of tea, Officer?"

Sergeant Pender grasped the mug with one hand and with the other covered the top. "It settles the nerves, sir."

"Commendable!" Chief Inspector Little turned and walked to the sink. After a moment of staring through the window at the small yard and brick wall, he muttered, "Lady Herriman is in shock. Goodness knows what it will do to Sir Sandoe when word gets to him. No doubt it will mean the end of this year's police ball... unless... Withers, where did you say Sir Sandoe was again?"

"Returning from Norwich, sir."

"Ah, sad news strikes hardest when one is toiling away from home." The chief inspector, motionless, continued to face the window. "This is a rather sticky wicket, a difficult business, indeed. But I'm sure there is a reasonable explanation."

It seemed like a strange way to proceed, but I knew from reading newspaper reports there was always a method to a great detective's madness.

The chief inspector said, "Sergeant, I consider Sir Sandoe a friend. He overdoes it; I've told him as much... at a business meeting in Norwich, I suppose?"

Sergeant Pender gave a little cough. "No, sir. At the races."

The chief inspector spun around. He reached for his top pocket then for his left side pocket, finally his right. He pulled out a ragged betting slip. "Knew it was in here somewhere. Now, I wonder if

Fancy Pants won, an insider tip from Sir Sandoe. Not that they've been much good of late."

Sergeant Pender took a quick gulp from his mug and said, "Sir, I've taken statements."

"Good." The chief inspector eased the betting slip back into his pocket. "There is no need to mention the whereabouts of Sir Sandoe in your notes. It is not relevant to today's events."

"Are you sure, sir?"

Chief Inspector Little tilted his chin upward. "Thanks to Lady Herriman, I have a full command of the facts. We know Miss Antoinette Sandoe disappeared around three years ago, believed to have run off with a disreputable fellow to America. We now know she never left the confines of these walls." He shook his head as if in disbelief. "I hope Sir Sandoe will find some relief in the knowledge his daughter's character remains intact."

Dolly said, "That will also be of great comfort to Lady Herriman."

Chief Inspector Little said, "Now I shall question the witnesses." He raised his index finger and pointed at me. "Mrs Mullins, can you walk me through your discovery."

Sergeant Pender coughed. "Sir, that is Miss Maggie Darling."

"Then who the devil is Mrs Mullins?"

Mrs Mullins raised her hand and, still full of plum wine, giggled, "That would be me, Sir Sherlock."

The chief inspector peered at the woman. "Ah, yes. Now tell me how you came to discover the body."

She let out a drunken giggle. "Gawd help us! Do you want me magnifying glass?"

Chief Inspector Little straightened. "What did you say?"

"I didn't discover no body. I discovered the person who found the body."

Chief Inspector Little gave her an incredulous stare. "What on earth are you babbling about, woman?"

Sergeant Pender said, "Miss Darling found the body, sir."

I raised my hand. "That's me."

The chief inspector's mouth dropped open. "You discovered the body?"

"That is so."

His forehead wrinkled. "On the bed, if I recall the facts of the case correctly."

"Under the blankets."

"Ah, yes." He closed his eyes as a child might to block out the scary dark. Then in a halting voice he said, "Did you notice anything unusual in the room?"

"No."

"Good, good." Now came his second question, once again asked in a halting voice. "Or on the bed?"

"No."

"Good, very good." The chief inspector's voice brightened. "What about the body? Anything strange about it?"

I said, "Perhaps you should take a look for yourself. I'm not an expert in such things."

The chief inspector's eyes narrowed. "Please answer my question. Was there anything strange about the body?"

"I didn't hang around to investigate. I'm not a police officer."

He changed the subject. "And the air, did it smell of anything unusual?"

"Mould, damp, and the like."

"But that is not unusual, is it?"

"No."

There was a pause while Chief Inspector Little looked slowly around, first at me, then at the other ladies sitting at the table and finally at Sergeant Pender. He touched his cheek. "Sergeant Pender, we can put this one away."

"We can, sir?"

"Have your report on my desk in the morning."

The sergeant took a swig from his mug. "What should I write, sir?"

"Good heavens, man, it is obvious. The eyewitness found nothing unusual about the body or surrounding area. Further, we believe the body is of Antoinette Sandoe. Of course, Dr Swensen will confirm. Now think, man. What do you think happened to the poor girl?"

"I dunno."

Chief Inspector Little lowered his angular brows. His squirrel-like expression became intense. "Antoinette wandered into the room and climbed the stairs. Do you see it?"

"Ah, yes, sir, that makes sense."

Chief Inspector Little smiled. "Now what does the bed tell us?"

"That she sat down, sir."

"Exactly! I'll make a detective of you yet." The chief inspector's eyes went wide, and he clapped his hands. "Antoinette sat and began to sing."

"Sing, sir?"

"Lady Herriman says she loved to croon popular songs sitting on her bed. Sad songs about things going wrong and people dying. I suspect when she finished singing, she lay down and fell asleep."

"And never woke up," added Sergeant Pender, helpfully.

"Not quite so fast, Officer. We first need to tackle the question as to why she entered the room."

"Righto, sir."

The chief inspector raised his index finger like a science professor about to make a key point. "We must remember Antoinette Sandoe was a lady. It doesn't take much to realise she entered the room for a little solitude and prayer. I suspect it was then she changed her mind about running away. Then after a little more singing and prayer, she found herself trapped in the room."

"Ah, yes, sir. I kind of see your logic... and there was a small hole at the bottom of the door. The door that led to the attic."

"A hole in the door, you say?"

"Yes, sir," said Sergeant Pender. "Rotten wood, tiny hole. Antoinette must have caused it in her desperate attempt to get out. But she was too slight a figure to shove the entire door open."

"Bingo! Add that to your report. I shall investigate the door before I leave." The chief inspector shook his head. "Nothing but a tragic accident. Once Dr Swensen has finished his examination, I'll pass on the report to the county coroner, and we'll close the case. Lady Herriman and Sir Richard Sandoe have been through quite enough turmoil."

Chapter 24

UNCLE TRISTAN PUT HIS foot against the pedal, and the old motorcar took off along the narrow lane, flinging up a trail of dust in its wake.

I jammed my feet against the floorboards, hands curled tight, with Swiftee clinging to my lap. What with the cider still sloshing around in my stomach, the discovery of Antoinette Sandoe's body, my new kitten, and the Norfolk countryside whistling by, I was in a daze.

Uncle Tristan wound his window down, tipped his head back, and let out a drunken roar. "This is the life, Maggie, can't beat the Norfolk countryside."

The road opened up before us. Green and brown fields, hedgerows with cattle grazing. It wasn't until Uncle Tristan slowed the motorcar on a tight bend that I spoke.

"I can't decide what to make of today. It's been so confusing."

Uncle Tristan turned to face me. "A wonderful day to leave the past."

I said, "Keep your eyes on the road, Uncle."

He yanked on the steering wheel. The motorcar swerved. "Tell me again about Lady Herriman and the body."

As he slowed the vehicle to a crawl, I recounted all that had happened. When I finished, he let out a long sigh, and a hint of apprehension entered his voice.

"Maggie, are you sure it is the body of Antoinette Sandoe?"

"Who else could it be?"

He shrugged and said in a wistful voice, "I don't know... "

The motorcar came to a stop while a herd of cattle crossed in front of us. The farmer gave a wave as he hurried the stragglers on.

Uncle Tristan said, "If it really is Miss Antoinette, things might be slow around Tristan's Hands for a while. I expect Sir Sandoe will put a hold on any hiring, at least until after the funeral and mourning period. I can pay your board at Mrs Rusbridger's for a week or two, but with this turn in events... maybe you should go back to London."

The thought had entered my mind. There were always jobs to be had in the capital city if you looked hard enough. The problem was wages were barely enough to cover your living costs. And there were the crowds and the noise. Here in Cromer, the air was fresh and everything so still. I'd been away for seventeen years and wasn't ready to go back.

But if Uncle Tristan wanted me to return... I said, "There is always Mr Pritchard's pie-and-mash shop."

Uncle Tristan let out an angry grunt. "On bended knee back into that dog's den, eh? I thought my sister made you of sterner stuff."

He was right. I said, "Mother brought me up to be independent, so did Father. No, I'm not ready to leave Cromer. I want to help you build the business."

Uncle Tristan's lips curved into a grin. "Very well. It is gruel for us both until our boat comes in."

"When do you think that will be?"

"I shall find an opportune time to speak with Sir Sandoe soon after Antoinette's body is laid to rest."

Uncle Tristan steered the motorcar around another tight bend. The road dipped down, running alongside a narrow stream. He said, "Did Chief Inspector Little give any word on his investigation?"

I let out a sigh. "The man is hardly Sherlock Holmes."

Uncle Tristan eased the motorcar up a steep incline. "It seems you have his number."

I said, "Do you know he will close the case tomorrow?"

"Thank God. That means the funeral will be this week. Only a few days on gruel, my girl!"

"The thing I don't understand," I said, speaking slowly as my thoughts formed, "is why the chief inspector didn't visit the body."

Uncle Tristan slammed on the brakes. "Why not?"

"Lumbago."

"Eh?"

"The chief inspector didn't want to climb the stairs on account of it. Anyway, he believes the death was a tragic accident. He might be right, but what if..." My voice trailed off. I wasn't ready to speculate just yet.

Uncle Tristan gave me a knowing look. "Maggie, this is Cromer where things get swept under the carpet. A young lad lost his feet last harvest. The official line is he was drunk, but I heard it was faulty machinery. The landed gentry get away with all sorts that would put the ordinary man behind bars. One rule for the rich and another for the poor. That has always been the way."

I said, "All I'm saying is that Chief Inspector Little should have ruled out all other possibilities before jumping to the conclusion that it was an accident."

Uncle Tristan put his foot on the gas. The motorcar shot forward. "Do you know Sir Sandoe didn't get along with his daughter?"

"That's not a surprise," I said, hanging on to the seat and Swiftee. The vehicle rocked from side to side. I stifled a sneeze. "The man's views are from the ancient past."

Uncle Tristan yanked the steering wheel to the right, narrowly avoiding a pothole. "They fought over their political differences, but that wasn't their biggest problem. Miss Antoinette Sandoe"—he spoke slowly like he thought I needed time to digest his words—"wasn't Sir Richard Sandoe's child."

Astonished, I said, "What are you saying?"

"Sir Richard was Lady Sandoe's second husband. Antoinette was her only child. Her first husband died in the war. Sir Richard married into Lady Sandoe's money."

The road levelled off. The motorcar picked up even more speed.

I said, "What happened to Lady Sandoe?"

"Vanished about five years ago. Local rumour says she was taken by Black Shuck on account of marrying beneath her status."

Chapter 25

I'D HEARD MANY STORIES of Black Shuck when I was a child. The tales recounted around an evening fire, in the dead of winter, involved a shaggy, black dog with fiery eyes. Black Shuck was responsible for uncountable mysteries in Norfolk.

And in my family too.

When Mother's apple pie went missing, Father said it was Black Shuck, and that everyone knows dogs have a sweet tooth. Then there was Father's ragged cloth cap. It vanished one night from the coat stand. Mother said Black Shuck took it for a dead squirrel and tossed it into the sea. Now Lady Sandoe had been taken by the creature, but that wasn't an opinion I could accept.

"Surely there was a police investigation?"

Uncle Tristan let out a cynical chuckle. "A flurry of activity over a week or two, but they never found any trace of her. There was more interest by the local constabulary in finding Albina's Hoard."

"Albina's what?"

"Ancient Roman treasure buried on the Bagington Hall estate. There was an article about it in the parish magazine. Poked around the estate after dark myself but didn't turn up anything but mud."

I feared Uncle had gold fever and changed the subject back to Lady Sandoe. "Did the police find a body?"

He shrugged. "The woman simply disappeared. It was as if Black Shuck devoured her, bones and all!"

"That is a rather odd coincidence," I said, my mind whirring. "Both mother and daughter dead in a handful of years."

Uncle Tristan took both hands off the steering wheel and waved them in the air as if it might help me understand his point. "Maggie, let's not jump to conclusions. We don't know what happened to Lady Sandoe. The woman might still be alive. She could be in America."

There wasn't much chance of that in my mind, but I said, "Uncle, keep your eyes on the road and hands on the steering wheel. Did Sir Sandoe inherit his wife's wealth?"

Uncle Tristan replied, "I don't know."

I'd read stories in London newspapers of husbands killing their wives for their money, with the help of corrupt police officers, and said, "Did the police investigate Lady Sandoe's disappearance?"

"Chief Inspector Little took personal charge."

I shook my head in shock. "Do you know the chief inspector is good friends with Sir Sandoe?"

Uncle Tristan nodded. "They are often together at the horse races. It is a small community. Everyone knows everyone else."

This didn't smell right. I said, "Don't you think his friendship might cloud his judgement as a police officer?"

"What are you saying?"

"The whole situation makes me uneasy. If it were natural causes, then so be it. But if there was foul play, Antoinette deserves justice."

It was as if my words were bolts of electricity. Uncle Tristan stopped the vehicle, flung open the motorcar door, and pranced back and forth at the side of the road waving his hands about as if on fire.

When he returned to the motorcar, he said, "Bravo, Maggie! You sound like your mother. My sister always had a keen sense of justice. Wrongdoings got under her skin, and her ideas to put things right always seemed to involve me and trouble! Now what are you saying?"

I knew what I thought, and so did Uncle, but I didn't want to say. "I don't know."

His eyes drifted skyward in thought. Then his voice dropped. "Maggie, you might be onto something."

Swiftee wriggled.

I sneezed.

Uncle slammed his hands on the dashboard.

I jumped.

"Maggie, you didn't ask me about my day."

"You made me jump for that?"

"Ask me?"

"Uncle!"

"Okay, I'll tell you anyway. Do you know Frank Perry?"

"I was there when he got into the scuffle with the gatekeeper."

"But did you see everything?"

I rolled my eyes and spoke in a deadpan tone. "Frank Perry climbed on the back of the truck and jumped off. Then he got into a scuffle with the gatekeeper. I saw the whole thing."

"You missed something."

"Don't be silly. I can even recall the words of George Edwards: 'We are 'ere to peaceable protest.' What on earth could I have missed?"

"When I worked as Lord Avalon, Man of Mystery, I learned to observe everything. Magicians have to see what others miss."

"I'm all ears."

"When Frank jumped off the truck, he crouched low and pulled something from his jacket pocket. I saw the flash of silver and kept my eyes focused." Uncle Tristan reached into his cape and yanked out a silver envelope. "I watched this flutter to the ground and picked it up during the scuffle with the gatekeeper's men."

I gaped at Uncle Tristan in astonished disbelief. "Sergeant Pender mentioned Frank had a letter for Sir Sandoe, but his pockets were empty!"

Uncle waved the envelope. "Well, here it is."

I snatched a hand at the envelope and missed. "What does it say?"

"Maggie! You can't expect me to open another man's private correspondence. I shall return it to Mr Frank Perry at the first available opportunity."

Chapter 26

THE NEXT MORNING, THERE was an excited buzz in the small dining room at the boarding house. Mrs Rusbridger flitted around the long single table with a tray of breakfast plates. Although there were only four guests, everyone talked at once and about one thing—the events at Bagington Hall.

I sat quietly, eating a bowl of porridge, while they continued their conversation.

"Did you hear," said a long-faced woman with a little sour mouth, "that the servant's room was filled with bodies. Wall to ceiling, like a church crypt."

"Oh my goodness," replied her companion, a stout woman with small eyes. "A gentleman close to Bagington Hall called out to me in the street yesterday evening. He mentioned the place has always been short of staff. Now I can see why. Did you know Sir Sandoe's wife disappeared a few years back?"

"Dear God!" The exclamation came from the long-faced woman with the little sour mouth. "Three shillings they'll find her body amongst the bones in the servant's room. Any takers?"

There were none.

"The whole thing is a disgrace!" The third woman, tall and elegant with full eyebrows, added, "There'll be no arrests, you know that, don't you? Sir Sandoe has the local constabulary in his back pocket. I doubt we'll even read about it in the newspapers. In a week it will have died down, in a month forgotten, and in a year the cover-up will be complete, and locals will put it down to Black Shuck."

There was a general murmur of agreement.

At this point, Mrs Rusbridger put down her tray, picked up a wooden spoon, and banged it on the table. "This 'ere is a respectable establishment. Lady Blackwood would 'ave it no other way. And that includes gossip and speculation. Such things are unladylike, and you should know better!"

The women were in their element and resented having their pleasure cut short.

"Mrs Rusbridger, we are just discussing the known facts," interjected the long-faced woman with the little sour mouth. "Not a word of gossip has passed any of our lips."

Mrs Rusbridger folded her thick arms. She shook her round face from side to side. Her saucers for eyes settled on me. "Now if you want to knows what happened yesterday, why don't you asks the person what discovered the body. She is sitting right here, all quiet eating her porridge."

Everyone's eyes turned in my direction. Mrs Rusbridger's shone the brightest. "Tell us what happened, love." She pulled out a seat and sat down. "Not that we are being nosy."

Oh bother!

I put down my spoon. The truth was I wanted to put the events of yesterday into the past. I wanted to forget about what I'd seen. I wanted to forget about the niggling sense of disquiet I felt about the death of Antoinette Sandoe and the disappearance of her mother.

I wanted nothing more to do with Bagington Hall. But with all eyes on me, there was no chance of that.

I said, "There is so little to tell; it is hardly worth the words."

The long-faced woman with the little sour mouth said, "That's what we all hoped, isn't it, ladies?"

"Yes," they cried as one.

The woman continued, "Start at the very beginning. Take your time, and don't leave anything out. That way, we can stop the spread of disreputable rumours."

When I'd finished and answered the many questions, Mrs Rusbridger stood up and hurried to the kitchen. She came back a few moments later and said, "Miss Darling is a wonderful young lady. She has given me a little kitten rescued from Bagington Hall." She held up Swiftee.

"Nice little fellow, isn't he?" said the tall, elegant woman with full eyebrows.

Mrs Rusbridger grinned. "And you'll never guess what he did last night." She didn't wait for an answer. "He caught a mouse!"

Chapter 27

I WASN'T EVEN HURRYING.

A weak sun shone between soaring banks of pale-white clouds. A blackbird cackled its alarm. I'd just stepped out of Mrs Rusbridger's boarding house, walked along the gravel path, and rounded a corner onto the lane.

I turned to gaze in the direction of the blackbird chirp, and without warning, a black dog bounded along the lane. It scurried towards me like a horse on the gallop. With quick foot movements I sidestepped the animal, and that was when Hilda Ogbern, pushing a cart of vegetables, chasing after the dog, flew out from behind a hedge, and it wasn't possible to adjust my feet in time.

The cart clattered into my legs, tipping me over. The vegetables scattered in every direction.

"Hullo, luv. Sorry about that," Hilda said as she reached out a hand to pull me to my feet. For a short dumpling of a woman, she had strong arms. "That new puppy will be the death of me. Dobbin, wait!"

The dog sat.

"Puppy! Why, he is huge," I said.

Hilda placed a hand on her hip. "That animal takes off like a greyhound, and there ain't a drop of pedigree in his bones." Her roguish face and bright, eager eyes glanced at me. "Miss Maggie Darling, ain't it?"

Working together, we righted the cart and repacked the vegetables. All the while, Hilda Ogbern talked with enthusiasm about nothing in particular—the warm weather, the state of the railways, training the puppy. "And Vicar Humberstone encourages me to let Dobbin run free."

"How so?" I asked.

"The vicar likes to leave 'im titbits in the graveyard. Claims Dobbin scares away the rats. Attract them more like!"

I could see by the eager gleam in her eyes there was news she was bursting to share, and it didn't involve the vicar, rats, or Dobbin's wayward nature.

At last, when everything was in order, Hilda said, "I'm on my way to Mrs Rusbridger's. Are you staying there?"

"For the moment," I replied. "It is a wonderful boarding house and very affordable. I'll stay for another week, at least."

Hilda rested her hands on the handle of the cart. "Me and Mrs Rusbridger are old friends, tell each other the news so we can keep up to date."

So that was it. There was something new on the Cromer gossip grapevine, and it didn't take a genius to work out what. I said, "Do you have news about Bagington Hall?"

"Aye, that would be it. Don't suppose there is much I can tell you, seeing as you found the body." She peered into my eyes as if trying to read my mind. "But I know something you don't know, and I'll put a shilling on that."

"Hilda, I'd take the bet, but I don't have a shilling to spare."

Hilda laughed. Again, the blackbird cackled its alarm. We all turned towards the sound.

"Dear me," Hilda muttered under her breath. "They say when the blackbird calls the alarm, they'll be a day of doom ahead."

Growing up in Cromer, I'd heard that and other superstitious Victorian mumblings. As far as I could discern, there wasn't a shred of truth in any of them.

"Oh, Hilda, that is nothing but an old wives' tale." I sneezed. "A modern woman like you should know better than repeating such nonsense."

Hilda folded her arms. After a long moment of silence, she said, "Looks like you are coming down with something."

I said, "I gave Mrs Rusbridger a new kitten. I'm allergic to cats."

"And chicken feathers," Hilda said, recalling our conversation on the train. "Oh, how I suffered terrible from that too when I first moved to the country. Not any longer though."

Now I was keen to hear how she'd overcome her allergies. I sneezed and said, "I'm all ears. Please tell me what you did. I'll do anything to get rid of this."

Hilda wagged a finger in my face. "Miss Darling, I'd like to tell you how I fixed the sneezing problem, but it's an old wives' tale, so I shan't bother."

"Now, listen, Hilda, you can't mention a cure and then snatch it away."

Hilda said, "But a modern woman like me has no business spreading Victorian old wives' tales."

I cleared my throat and said, "Point taken. Now are you going to tell me, or do I have to sneeze it out of you?"

Hilda unfolded her arms. "Now listen good to this old wife and her tale. To fix the sneezes, take two tablespoons of apple cider vinegar with a glass of water and a squeeze of lemon juice. Mind you, take it three times a day, and you'll be as right as rain."

The blackbird cackled another warning cry. We both looked in its direction. Dobbin's front paws stretched high on the trunk of an oak tree.

"Down, Dobbin," yelled Hilda. The dog turned its head, seemed to get the message, and sat. Hilda placed a hand on my arm. "Now, Miss Darling, why don't you come with me back to the boarding house. That way I can tell you the news at the same time as Mrs Rusbridger."

Chapter 28

ON THE DOORSTEP OF the boarding house, Hilda tied up the puppy to her vegetable cart then pushed open the front door. I followed her inside.

The guests had retired to their rooms, and Mrs Rusbridger was in the kitchen, arms deep in cold water washing dishes, pots, and pans.

"Hullo, hullo!" said Hilda.

Mrs Rusbridger's round face turned from the pots, the room still exuding the pungent flavours of breakfast. Not a word was exchanged for several seconds. Gradually, recognition came to her large, round eyes. She straightened up, wiped her hands on an old rag, and cleared her throat.

"News of Bagington Hall?"

"Aye," replied Hilda. "That would be about right."

Mrs Rusbridger's eyes twitched like a bird eyeing a worm. "Get to it, woman. What is it?"

"Better sit down, and I'll take the weight off me feet as well."

Hilda took her time sitting down, clearly enjoying being at the centre of attention.

I followed her to a seat, keen to hear the news.

Hilda began slow, like a comedian warming up the crowd. "Knows Mrs Garfield?"

"Of course I knows Mrs Garfield," huffed Mrs Rusbridger. "The two of us went to school together, and she works for Dr Swensen. I've known the woman all my life. Now spit it out."

"Aye, that's right, it must 'ave slipped my mind, what with the shock of the news." Hilda's words came out slow as if she was tasting every syllable. "Just got back from speaking with Mrs Garfield. Dr Swensen is at the bottle again."

"What for, this time?"

"On account of the Bagington Hall body."

"What about the body?"

"Belongs to Antoinette Sandoe."

"Dear God," said Mrs Rusbridger, her voice barely a whisper. "That's what everyone thought. Poor lass. Better have a tot of brandy."

Mrs Rusbridger hurried to an overhead cupboard, rustled around, and came back with three china cups and a half-empty bottle of brandy. She sloshed it liberally into each cup.

Hilda took a long sip and said, "The funeral is tomorrow at eleven."

"I'll be there to pay my respects," said Mrs Rusbridger, her eyes now the size of dinner plates.

"But that's not the end of it." Hilda's voice cackled like the alarm call of a blackbird. "Mrs Garfield says Dr Swensen found a big ole long-handled dagger sticking out of her chest. It had the letters XOT scratched in the handle. Antoinette Sandoe was murdered!"

Chapter 29

"COMMAND TO THE GRAVE"—Vicar Humberstone raised his eyes to the heavens and then turned to the gathered crowd—"the body of your servant, Antoinette Sandoe."

Lady Herriman stood side by side with Sir Richard Sandoe who, stiff and pale, held the coffin cord tight with both hands. Behind them were a gaggle of Bagington Hall workers and villagers.

It seemed the entire village had turned out. I'd only been in town a few days, but already I could pick out a few faces. Dolly Trimmings stood next to Withers, who wore a black suit with a silk top hat that shone with the polish of a well-kept boot. His white-gloved hands and thin sword cane gave him the look of a Victorian gentleman. Hilda Ogbern and Mrs Rusbridger stood a little way back from the main crowd, their heads close as if exchanging confidential information.

I recognised Boots and the gatekeeper amongst a group of flat-capped men. Mrs Mullins had an arm over the shoulder of her niece, Rose. And tall, broad-shouldered Sergeant Pender watched with hooded eyes along with a group of constables, a little way behind Chief Inspector Little.

I stood near the back of the crowd with Uncle Tristan's arm about my shoulder. Memories of Mother's funeral flooded my mind. The sun shone brightly on that day. It had cast long shadows on the dreary headstones. Today, that same sun shone in a cloudless sky. I felt like I was in a dreadful dream with everything moving in slow motion as if I had suddenly been tossed into a thick syrup.

Uncle Tristan whispered, "Maggie, promise me you'll go easy on yourself. Don't let the memories of your mother's send-off stir you up. If you break down and cry, I'll be rolling on the ground bawling too. And neither of us want that."

Trust Uncle Tristan to say just the right thing to make me smile. "Promise," I said, wiping moisture from my eye. "I'll only allow a teardrop or two."

Vicar Humberstone glanced towards the church clock as if wishing the whole dreadful thing was over. "Antoinette was a very special young lady. She had a particular interest in languages and local history. I read with great anticipation her musings on the location of Albina's Hoard printed in the parish magazine." He let out an apologetic sigh and with hands raised said, "Ashes to ashes, dust to dust..."

Lady Herriman stepped forward, lifted her black veil with one hand, and wiped her dim eyes with a silk handkerchief. In a high, tremulous tone, she said, "Poor Antoinette! How I have missed our evening Bible readings, your singing, and our chats about your future. Your mother loved you. If only she hadn't married a scoundrel who poisoned her mind."

The vicar moved towards Lady Herriman, thought better of it, and stopped.

"It wasn't your fault, Antoinette. You know that, don't you," cried Lady Herriman to the open grave as she pulled the veil back over her face. "That man masquerading as your father ought to be horsewhipped!"

Dolly Trimmings placed an arm around Lady Herriman's trembling shoulder. "This way, madam," Dolly whispered. "Let's sit in the motorcar a while and rest."

Lady Herriman shook free of her grip. "I'm not some feeble, old woman! No, I've stared death in the face and won." She lifted the veil, eyes blazing at Sir Sandoe. "At least now Antoinette can rest in peace for eternity."

"This way, madam," Dolly repeated. She took a gentle grip on Lady Herriman's arm and led her away from the open grave.

Vicar Humberstone coughed, adjusted his ceremonial robe. His head tilted skyward, eyelids dropped as if in private prayer, but his eyes followed Lady Herriman until she disappeared behind a stone monument. "Sir Sandoe, please."

Sir Richard Sandoe responded with a bleak smile, his hands opening. The cord dropped. It hit the top of the coffin with a thud.

Uncle squeezed me tight against his shoulder.

I wiped tears from my eyes.

Vicar Humberstone turned, and with solemn steps strode away from the grave towards the church entrance.

Sir Sandoe remained very still for a moment, staring into the grave. With a slow movement, he reached into his jacket pocket, retrieved a hip flask, and took a long hard swig. Then he turned and walked away.

Two gravediggers set to work with their shovels.

Uncle Tristan's arm slipped from my shoulder.

The crowd turned away. As they broke up into small groups, I watched Chief Inspector Little approach Sir Sandoe. There was deference in his step, a slight stoop to his shoulders as if he were in the presence of royalty. Sir Sandoe extended his hand. The two men shook.

The chief inspector muttered something into Sir Sandoe's ear. I was too far away to hear the words, but Sir Sandoe seemed to visibly relax as if relieved of some great tension, and I thought I saw a flicker of a smile on his long, narrow bovine face.

Chapter 30

"THIS IS A TERRIBLE business," said Boots. He rocked back and forth from foot to foot, his small eyes occasionally gazing at the gravediggers. "I mean, Lady Sandoe goes missing; Tommy Crabapple loses his feet, and now this!"

I stood under the shade of a large oak tree with a small group of Bagington Hall workers and Uncle Tristan. A squirrel hopped from branch to branch casting nervous glances at the humans below. The soft sound of the shovels against dirt and strained grunts of the gravediggers carried in the still air.

"It's the devil's work," uttered the gatekeeper. "There be no doubt about it."

Uncle Tristan waved his arms about, palms out. "Man, what are you talking about? All this devil talk is ridiculous."

"Aye, that's what Miss Antoinette used to say," muttered the gatekeeper. "But look at her now. The curse will be on you next if you don't mind your words."

We gazed at the grave. The diggers worked fast, shovelling soft soil into the cavernous hole where the remains of Antoinette lay in a sealed casket. At that moment, as we all stood in silence and watched, there seemed to be a profound truth in the gatekeeper's words.

"It's the devil's work; make no bones about it," again muttered the gatekeeper.

This was too much for Uncle Tristan. He folded his arms and said, "Nonsense! Now let's not be having any of that talk. What happened to Miss Antoinette was an act of wickedness—"

"Isn't that but another name for the devil?" interrupted the gatekeeper.

Uncle Tristan ignored his interjection and continued, "But what on earth has it to do with the disappearance of Lady Sandoe or the accident of Tommy Crabapple?"

"They are related as night is to day," said the gatekeeper, his voice as low as the gentle breeze. "Who is the master of Bagington Hall?"

"And Sir Sandoe runs the place like the devil himself," added Boots.

"With a temper to match," said the gatekeeper.

"Come now," said Uncle Tristan. "Sir Sandoe would never raise a hand against anyone."

"Then you ain't been the object of his temper," replied the gatehouse keeper, "cos if you were, you'd know better. The man is like a lunatic let loose from the asylum when he's angry."

"Vicious temper and as cunning as a fox," added Boots. "Why else would he spread a rumour about Miss Antoinette running off to America when he knows it ain't true? What other rumours has he started? That don't sound like no gentleman to me."

But Uncle Tristan would not back down. I feared the prospect of gold may have warped his mind. He said, "In my dealings, he has been nothing but a gentleman."

I remembered my first meeting with Sir Sandoe on the train to Cromer and felt differently. Yes, he'd served his country, and he was part of the landed gentry, but the quality of his opinions did not differ from those die-hard Victorian men I'd met in the pie-and-mash shop. Take away the title, the money, and what remained? A bigoted little man who was afraid of the changing times.

Uncle Tristan said, "Sir Sandoe has been gracious to me. There are certain opportunities for which he has aided my progress. Take, for example, my staffing agency. It was his idea." He puffed up his chest and gave his cape a swirl. "Do you seriously believe Sir Sandoe knew his own daughter lay rotting in that disused room?"

"Miss Antoinette was not his flesh and blood," said Boots.

"And it's his house, he should 'ave known," added the gatekeeper.

"And what justice does he get?" said Boots. "I tell you, it ain't right."

"Careful what you say," said Uncle Tristan. "If it were not for Sir Sandoe, you'd be unemployed. I know it upsets you, but today is about Miss Antoinette Sandoe. Can we respect that?"

The men fell into an uneasy quiet.

The sound of the shovels was suddenly very different. No longer a hollow clang but a solid thud. We turned to watch the gravediggers toss on the final sods of earth.

"All done here," cried one gravedigger.

"A crying shame," muttered the other. "And at her funeral. Can you believe it?"

"Aye, I believe it. Not that I wouldn't mind a bit of gold, but I'd not touch anything Sir Sandoe had his hand in. What type of devil tries to sell shares at his own daughter's funeral? Bloody hot out here. Let's get inside and 'ave a cup of tea."

Uncle Tristan's jaw tightened. He rubbed a hand over the back of his neck, his eyes narrowing as if a new truth had suddenly entered his mind.

Chapter 31

IT WAS GETTING TOWARDS twelve o'clock when Uncle Tristan bounded in the direction of the last sighting of Sir Sandoe. He took enormous prancing strides, head tilted skyward, eyes fierce.

For a second too long I hesitated, unwilling to call out or to venture after him, yet unwilling to linger in the shade of the oak tree with Boots, the gatekeeper, and other Bagington Hall workers.

It wasn't until Uncle Tristan disappeared behind a tree, I hurried after him. I thought about gold, Peru, and the gravediggers' words. If there were no mines in Peru, no shares and no gold, I wanted to be there for Uncle when that exceedingly comfortless news broke.

I cut through a rough part of the graveyard. Overgrown tufts of grass stretched between the headstones with untidy beds of weeds where it once had grown azaleas. The wind picked up, blowing strongly through the tall oak trees, making their leaves rustle and crackle like the embers of a dying fire. I could see Uncle's cape as he turned a sharp corner beside the church.

Near the entrance, I stopped. Vicar Humberstone talked to Withers. He jabbed his fingers into the man's chest, shook his fist, and then slapped the man on the back. All the while, the butler's head hung like a wilted flower needing water.

I stood watching them. The vicar's face contorted as he spoke, his eyes locked on the drooped head of Withers. I thought he looked like a boxing coach in the corner urging his fighter on for another round.

"What on earth?"

Keeping out of sight, I walked closer and continued to watch from behind a tall stone monument. The vicar's mouth was working hard, his lips drawn back exposing two rows of very large uneven teeth, slightly tarnished. But all that carried were snippets of words.

Curiosity got the better of me. With the stealth of Swiftee, I edged closer, careful to keep from their direct line of sight.

"Withers, it is not your fault." Vicar Humberstone's voice carried on the breeze. He spoke fast, in the tone of a parent comforting a child. "Dear me, it is not your fault at all."

Withers tapped his sword cane on the bare dirt. "But you—"

The vicar raised a hand, cutting off Withers. "Good man, we'll have none of that! Do you hear me? None of that, at all."

Withers persisted. "Vicar, it is just that my hands are—"

The vicar grabbed the man by his shoulders. "Leave Chief Inspector Little to his job. Focus on your work. From all accounts, you run Bagington Hall with an iron rod. Don't spare it; the workers will thank you, as I thank you for your continued support of our parish church."

Withers bobbed his head up and down, a white-gloved hand resting on his top hat. "Yes, you are right."

The vicar said, "I'm sure they'll track down the culprit—"

Withers interrupted, his voice a jangling ball of nerves. "Miss Antoinette disappeared three years ago. Surely, all the clues are long gone."

"And when they catch him, he'll swing for it."

Withers said, "Do you think so?"

"Now, man, you can't blame yourself for what has happened. There is no reason for you to feel guilty because you ordered the old chambermaid's quarters to be sealed and painted over three years ago. How were you to know Miss Antoinette Sandoe's body lay within? But keep that to yourself. No need to share it with the world, now, is there?"

The words appeared to galvanise Withers, for his shoulders went back, neck straightened, and once again, his posture was that of the master rather than servant.

"Vicar Humberstone, all I request is you add myself, Sir Sandoe, and Her Ladyship to your daily prayers. Will the usual compensation be adequate?"

"Indeed. I shall do as you requested," said the vicar. "In terms of compensation, I intend to do a spot of bowmanship this afternoon at Bagington Hall. I'd like a partridge for supper. Will the gamekeeper be occupied elsewhere?"

Withers touched the tip of his top hat with the sword cane. "Sir, you have free range over my land." He gave a slight nod of the head, his voice dropping to a low murmur. "The coast will be clear until six."

Chapter 32

"WHAT IN HEAVEN'S NAME are you doing?"

A firm hand gripped my shoulder.

I spun around.

Dolly Trimmings stared back.

"I... er... well..." I kept my voice low as I fumbled for words, my eyes wide with embarrassment.

"Is that you, Miss Darling? Oh Gawd, yes, yes, it is you!" Dolly placed a thick finger to her wide hippopotamus mouth. "Eaves-dropping, eh? Good for you. Only way to find out what's going on around here."

I hunched my shoulders and shifted my feet, trying to stop the flush I could feel on my cheeks. Then I collected myself, straight-ened my shoulders, and whispered, "Not intentionally, I was—"

"Stuff and nonsense," Dolly whispered. "Withers worries me to death, Miss Darling; he really does."

"Splendid," said the vicar, giving Withers a slap on the back. "A wonderful day for it."

"Indeed it is, Vicar Humberstone," replied Withers.

Dolly's birdlike eyes twitched towards the voices. "Withers is up to something. Do you know what they were talking about?"

Before I answered, Withers looked in our direction. If our presence surprised him, it did not show on his face. The man raised his top hat like a Victorian gentleman and tapped the sword cane on the ground. The vicar followed his gaze. His ruddy complexion seemed to deepen as he rubbed a hand over his heavy moustache.

In a voice that was barely a whisper, Vicar Humberstone said, "Well, hello, Dolly and Miss Darling."

Instantly, I was on the alert. Was the vicar testing how far his voice travelled and how much we might have overheard?

I was about to say, Pardon, can you speak up? when Dolly said, "How do, Vicar? I just got 'ere, but Miss Darling has been watching you two miscreants for quite a while. Ain't that so?"

The sight of two piercing sets of male eyes, with their cold, hard stares, produced in me a moment of dread. The skin on my face tingled. I could feel it stretching tight over my cheeks as I forced a smile. For some seconds I could neither think nor speak. When I began to think, I thought very quickly, and my subconscious and conscious mind worked together. But what they came up with was hardly worth the effort.

In a thin voice I said, "Gentlemen, I was looking for Mr Harbottle. Have you seen him?"

Withers and the vicar stared back with unblinking eyes.

Now my face did a passable imitation of a beetroot.

I tried again. "I believe Mr Harbottle came this way; did you see him?"

The sun dipped behind a cloud. The chatter of squirrels sounded out above the peace of the early afternoon. Neither Withers nor the vicar moved. For a few moments, it seemed they would stand there all day, like so many of the stone monuments scattered about the church graveyard.

"Miss Darling," said Dolly, breaking the silence. "I have been thinking that you really ought to give a little subscription to the parish magazine."

"But—" I murmured.

"We ought not to think of ourselves," interrupted the vicar. "Cromer is a small village. Our local magazine is in need of extra help. Can I put you down, Miss Darling?"

The skin tightened on my face. "I'd be delighted."

Vicar Humberstone smiled, but it did not extend to his piercing, bright eyes. "Then I shall put you down for five shillings a week. That seems fair, doesn't it?"

Before I could object, Dolly put a thick hand on my arm. "Lady Herriman would like a word with you. Come, she is waiting in her motorcar."

Chapter 33

DOLLY AND I STROLLED towards the Daimler Landaulette parked on the verge a short distance from the gates of the ancient, grey-stoned Saint Magdalene church. She chattered almost without taking a breath, but her voice seemed to me, high pitched and forced.

At the motorcar door, Dolly stopped abruptly and made warning signals with her eyes. Then she raised a hand to her mouth simulating a cup. Her Ladyship had been at the bottle. I stared at the curtained windows and drew myself up stiffly. Where was Uncle Tristan?

Dolly tapped the glass.

"Come," came the voice of Lady Herriman.

"Miss Darling is here for an audience with you, madam."

Lady Herriman gave a slight nod as I settled into the seat.

It was like a luxury hotel room on wheels. All elegant wood, waxed leather, and exquisite touches. The Daimler Landaulette was top of the line and a far cry from Uncle Tristan's bone-shaking, old banger. But the motor vehicle's exquisiteness paled into nothingness at the strong scent of alcohol that infused the still air. It oozed from the polished wood, rose from the shiny pelt, and hung about Lady Herriman like the boozy whiff of hops shrouds a brewery.

Quickly, I thought about the best way to play this. I decided to stick with compliments and humble pie. I caught my breath and clenched my hands, curling the edges of my lips upward into a pleasant smile.

Lady Herriman peered out from under thick-pencilled eyebrows, her face stiff with pale powder. In her hand, she held an oversized goblet. And next to her, leaning against the door, were a hand mirror, a leather briefcase, and an old hunting rifle.

"You may leave now," Lady Herriman said to Dolly. "This will only take five minutes. Please tell Withers I am ready to return to Bagington Hall."

Dolly nodded, gave me a wink, and withdrew from the vehicle.

After the door eased shut, Lady Herriman placed the goblet in a little holder and said, "A most trying day." From her mouth came the stench of aged wine mingled with sour milk. My stomach lurched.

I turned away.

"I can see it has affected you too, child." She reached out a hand and tapped my knee. The flesh on her face had a wasted and sandpaper appearance. "Death strikes at will and where it chooses. Nevertheless, it is always a shock."

I lowered my eyes, held my breath, and said, "Lady Herriman, I am sorry for your loss."

"Antoinette has left a hole in my heart. One wonders how it continues to beat." She reached into her handbag, pulled out her lorgnette spectacles, picked up the hand mirror, and surveyed herself under lowered eyelids. "Do you think the strain of it has aged me?"

I played the compliment card. "To lose a loved one would age anyone."

Her thin, wasted fingers bedecked in jewellery touched her hollow cheeks. "So you think I look older?"

"Very tired," I said, wondering how it was possible to look any more ancient. "And in need of relaxation."

"Yes, yes, you are right. If only Sir Sandoe didn't keep me caged up like a museum exhibit." Again, she scrutinised herself in the mirror, raising her chin and slightly pursing her thin lips. "Do you think I am too old to remarry?"

I shifted in my seat. "Well... love is eternal; isn't that what they say?"

"Oh my, such wise words for one so young. Reminds me of my time in France. Have you been to Paris?"

"No, Your Ladyship, only London." I tried to sound like Withers. Her Ladyship seemed to relish that sort of treatment.

"I suppose," she said, putting down the mirror, picking up the goblet, and staring into my eyes, "you should like to see a little of France?"

A thought crept slowly into my mind. I'd seen that look in Lady Herriman's eyes in many a man and woman in the pie-and-mash shop. Despite the hustle and bustle of running a large estate, she was lonely. And there was something else, but I couldn't think of the word.

"Yes, I should very much like to see France one day," I said, feeling a twinge of sadness for her. I'd made of point of making conversation with the patrons of Mr Pritchard's pie-and-mash shop. I paid particular attention to the elderly. They seemed to live in the past and were always in need of a little cheer. There and then I resolved to offer the same kindness to Her Ladyship.

Lady Herriman said, "When I was in Paris back in eighteen seventy-three, they said I had the look of the Mona Lisa. You have seen da Vinci's portrait, I take it?"

"Yes, madam. It is a masterpiece."

"Monsieur Bonhomme was quite taken aback by the resemblance. He insisted I visit his studio every day during my visit."

I thought back to my stay at Bagington Hall. I'd seen several portraits of Lady Herriman, all when she was much younger and dressed in hunting gear. I said, "Did Monsieur Bonhomme paint the pictures hanging in your private antechamber?"

Lady Herriman raised her right wrist. A gold bracelet jangled.

"Monsieur Bonhomme ran an exquisite jewellery studio off the Champs-Élysées. I believe this little bangle is one of his."

"Ah, I see it all now," I said then added, "Gold suits your skin tone."

"And diamonds too. I have a trunk full of Monsieur Bonhomme's trinkets from that vacation." Lady Herriman paused, reached for her goblet, and took a long slow drink. "Tell me, do you see the Mona Lisa in me?"

"Why... yes! Now you mention it... both you and the masterpiece... have eyes... I mean... there is a certain similarity around the eyes."

"Oh, that is so kind. Withers often compliments me on that feature." Her lips curved into a self-indulgent smile. "He even said you and I might be mistaken as sisters."

Not bloody likely, I thought, but said, "Isn't it fascinating how our physical features carry across the generations."

Lady Herriman put the lorgnette spectacles to her face and stared hard for several seconds.

"Oh dear, I would like very much to find the resemblance Withers speaks of. Your features are far from that of a da Vinci masterpiece, and you require some serious skincare. For a girl not yet in her twenties, your pallor is aged."

My jaw tightened. I looked down at my hands.

Lady Herriman said, "Never mind, child. We can't all be raging beauties. Take half a cup of donkey's milk daily, and things should improve. If you don't take care, you'll look like a prune in ten years!"

Disturbed! That was the word. Lady Herriman was lonely and disturbed. It was as if she'd been hypnotised and was living in a dream.

I said, "Donkey's milk... yes... that sounds... interesting... Do you use it yourself?"

"In our little audiences, I shall share with you all the beauty tips I would've liked to have given my niece."

A dissenting bell rang distantly in my mind. I rubbed my hands together for a moment, wondering what she meant by "our little audiences."

Lady Herriman let out a sigh, put the lorgnette spectacles down, and said, "Miss Darling, I've reviewed the documents you gave me. They are all in order."

Relieved her mind had drifted away from beauty tips, and we were onto the purpose for the audience, I said, "Tristan's Hands will be delighted to serve you and your household. Is there anything else you or Sir Sandoe should like to know?"

"Don't be ridiculous," snapped Lady Herriman. "Sir Sandoe has no part in the running of the household or the hiring of domestic staff. That is my responsibility and mine alone."

"Oh, I see."

"Sir Sandoe's responsibilities are that of the head of the estate—the grounds, farmland, buildings, and so on. I'm in charge of all domestic matters."

She reached into the leather case, shuffled through a pile of papers, placed her lorgnette spectacles to her face, and read in silence. After a moment, she looked up. "All that remains is to agree on a suitable date for payment and for Mr Harbottle to supply the required staff. But let's not discuss those details today. I'd like to invite you to dinner on Friday."

My first thought was this is amazing. I could barely hold my excitement. I'd secured the deal. And to top it off, a celebratory meal at Bagington Hall. It was a good feeling. Then I thought of Uncle Tristan, what he would wear, and how I'd keep him from annoying Her Ladyship. That wouldn't be easy, but I'd remind him gruel would be back on the menu if he messed up.

I said, "Thank you. Uncle Tristan will be delighted to attend the—"

"Not Mr Harbottle. Just you, child. How does roast swan with buttered potatoes sound? Queen Victoria swore by it. The leg is particularly tender."

The dissenting bell rang out in full alarm. "Roast... swan?"

Lady Herriman reached out a hand and pulled back the curtain. "Things are going to change around here. The death of Miss Antoinette has clarified my mind. Dolly, my chambermaid, is getting long in the tooth, and I don't like to say it, but the woman has a drinking problem."

Chapter 34

THE SHOUTS OF UNCLE Tristan drifted from the churchyard as I stepped from the Daimler Landaulet. I stopped still on the verge by the grey-stoned wall that ran around Saint Magdalene then pivoting, hurried to the wrought-iron gates.

From the entrance, I could see a great sweeping vista from the ancient stone church to the tall mossed monuments and headstones, both worn and new, but no Uncle Tristan.

Unlike London, where people hurried away after a funeral, here in Cromer, little groups milled about. The glorious weather played a part, and everyone wanted to make a day of it. Withers, in his Victorian gentleman's dress and sword cane, strode like a lord, along a narrow track. Dolly scurried at his heels. Before our paths crossed, I turned my back on the vista to look at the Daimler Landaulette. Through a pulled-back curtain, Lady Herriman peered out. She gave a regal wave of the hand. I waved back.

"Why do I get myself roped into these things," I muttered. "It must be some personality defect."

Again, I scanned the churchyard and frowned.

"Maggie, Maggie, Maggie!"

From a narrow path that dropped away behind a large stone monument, I saw the edge of Uncle Tristan's cape. It fluttered like a tatty flag in the quickening breeze. There was another burst of shouts, and Uncle Tristan appeared from behind an oak tree.

"Over here!" I called.

Uncle Tristan ran towards me with giant prancing steps, the Victorian cape trailing behind like a dragnet and far too heavy for such a bright and sunny day.

"Uncle, I'm here for you," I cried, fearful of the worst. I'd let him tell me all about the gold mine being nothing more than a mirage, or that they'd only discovered dust or a thousand and one other ways that Sir Sandoe's investment had turned out to be a worthless sham. Then when things seemed to be at their bleakest, I'd tell him of our new contract with Bagington Hall. Uncle and I might not be dining like royalty, but gruel would at least be off the menu.

As Uncle Tristan drew closer, I noticed his expression. His eyes were wide, nostrils dilated, and lips curved upward.

He was smiling.

"Maggie, ha-ha-ha, Maggie!"

He came to a full stop and made a bow. Visibly hot and out of breath, he said, "Oh, darling Maggie, if only you knew what wonders await us. Not next year, not next month, not next week, but right here and now!"

That was not what I was expecting. Nor did I expect Uncle Tristan to gather the cape above his skinny knees and cavort in circles with more energy than Hilda Ogbern's new puppy, Dobbin.

"Hooray, ha-ha-ha, hooray!"

Before I could protest, he swept me up in his skinny arms, and we twirled around the tombstones.

Dancing at a funeral might have been reasonable in some exotic foreign land, but here in Cromer, it was not the done thing. And I didn't want to draw the attention of Sir Sandoe.

"Uncle! Have you lost your mind? This isn't a London dance hall. Remember, today is about Miss Antoinette's send-off."

The words had the intended effect. Uncle Tristan stopped, doubled over to catch his breath, and said, "Miss Antoinette didn't mind a bit of dancing now and then. She had a good voice too and was a lot of fun." He rubbed his chin. "I've been looking all over for you. Where have you been?"

"With Lady Herriman," I said with a hint of annoyance.

"Another audience, huh?"

"Her Ladyship has reviewed our papers and finds them acceptable. Uncle, Bagington Hall is Tristan's Hands first client."

Uncle clapped his hands. "Now all we have to do is find people to fill Her Ladyship's staffing needs, and everything will be tickety-boo."

I said, "Did you speak with Sir Sandoe?"

"Only a few snatched minutes."

"Is everything lost?"

Uncle placed his hands on his hips. "This damn gold business has me disturbed."

"The money, Uncle, is it all gone?"

"I asked for my initial investment back."

"So there is nothing left?"

Uncle Tristan spoke as if to himself. "Sir Sandoe is old fashioned, but a gentleman in an oddly Victorian way."

I wasn't so sure. "But did Sir Sandoe agree to give your money back?"

"No."

Rattled, I gulped. "I'm sorry."

It didn't come as a shock. The London newspapers were full of reports of investment scandals in the Americas where investors lost everything. It seemed gold mining in Peru was just another of those empty treasure troves. What I couldn't understand was why Uncle Tristan had a big grin on his face.

I said, "There is more. Please do tell."

"Sir Sandoe has discovered another mine in Peru and is selling shares in that also."

"There are two mines, now?" I gave Uncle Tristan a grim look.

"It is so new he hasn't yet informed his backers in London."

"The gold mines are multiplying like bunny rabbits," I said acidly.

Uncle Tristan said, "Sir Sandoe has opened investment in the second mine to locals. That's why he was selling shares today."

"Do you think," I said, speaking with care, "that a man who tries to sell shares to gravediggers at his daughter's funeral can be fully trusted?"

Uncle Tristan tilted his head back and let out a belly laugh. "That is why I asked for my money back."

"But you said he refused to return your original investment."

"That's right." Uncle Tristan was still grinning. "Maggie, Sir Sandoe insisted on returning my money with an additional ten per cent on top!"

For once in my life, I was speechless. I just stared at Uncle Tristan, mouth agape, eyes wide.

Uncle Tristan said, "I almost told Sir Sandoe to keep some money back and invest in both mines, but I fear I may have put too many eggs in a single basket."

"The man is returning your original investment plus ten per cent?"

"And the bank cheque will be in my hands on Friday. I shall pick it up from him personally at Bagington Hall." Uncle Tristan placed a hand on his cheek. "Maggie, I have thought it all through very carefully, nothing out of place, nothing left to chance. When Sir Sandoe announces the discovery, I'll rush in and buy. Until then, I'll keep the cash in my pocket."

There was nothing I could say, so I continued to listen.

Uncle Tristan glanced warily over his shoulder. "Even better news, Sir Sandoe has agreed to advance your wages in full for the next year. The days of gruel for breakfast, lunch, and dinner are over before we've taken our first bite!"

I gave Uncle Tristan a big hug. Things had taken a turn for the better, and at a funeral of all places. But I didn't mention the faint trace of concern about Miss Antoinette's death that nagged at me: soft but persistent like the first drops of a spring thunderstorm. Whatever the outcome of the gold mining in Peru or Tristan's Hands, I would use every opportunity to dig into her death, leastways as a thank you for our good fortune, and because she deserved justice.

Chapter 35

WE TRAVELLED DOWN FROM Cromer in Uncle Tristan's motorcar that Friday. By the time we got to Bagington Hall, the sun was shining low in a clear blue western sky. But the air, chilled by the sea, came salty and stinging like a sudden hard slap across the cheeks.

Gone were the tablecloths; red, white, and blue bunting; and flags of my earlier visit. Four women huddled under an oak tree. A dozen cloth-capped men, hunched with heads down against the wind, marched in a tight circle in front of the gates. They carried signs demanding fair pay for fair wages and let out the occasional shout. I recognised none of the demonstrators, but they looked like local farmhands.

"There's no telling how long this strike will drag on," said Uncle Tristan, pulling the motorcar to a stop on the verge. "I shall speak with a few of the men. When this is all settled, they'll want work, and Tristan's Hands needs people. And in case things turn very sour, I shall cash Sir Sandoe's cheque as soon as he delivers it to me this afternoon."

I stayed in the car, sinking deep into the soft seat. The gatekeeper, hands on hips, spoke with two police officers. The taller, I recognised as Sergeant Pender. The other was a weedy, young constable, in a dingy uniform frayed at the elbows, shiny in the knees, with shabby, heavy boots that were once black.

"Afternoon, Sergeant Pender and Constable Lutz." The gate-keeper's deep voice carried in the still, frigid air. "Things have been quiet all day."

I closed my eyes and tried not to think back to the last time I'd visited this place. But I couldn't shake the image of the desiccated body of Miss Antoinette nor the feeling that something was off about Bagington Hall.

The upcoming dinner with Lady Herriman caused the acid to bubble in my stomach. I doubted the menu would be to my tastes. The woman was odd. But as Uncle had said, "We have to appease her until we get new clients. Then we will be home free."

An irate tapping on the side window caused me to bolt stiff upright.

"Hullo, luv!" The roguish face of Hilda Ogbern peered in through the side window alongside Dobbin, her puppy. "Saw your uncle and thought you'd be nearby." She tugged the motorcar door open. "Since you're here, you may as well join us. I'll introduce you to a few ladies; they are good workers."

Despite the chill, I cheerfully followed her to the group of women who stood shielded from the wind under an oak tree. Tristan's Hands needed domestic workers, and I needed a diversion from my thoughts about Lady Herriman.

After introductions, Hilda said, "My Harold's come out on strike, on account of Sir Sandoe. Don't know how long we'll last without his money, but the whole village is up in arms."

I said, "About pay and conditions?"

Hilda said, "Miss Antoinette!"

"Pardon?"

"First, His Lordship's wife goes missing, now the daughter. And what have the police done?"

"Nothing," the gathered women said as one.

Hilda jabbed a pudgy finger in the air and repeated the cry of the crowd. "A big fat zero, as far as we can see. The men work this land hard for next to nothing, but when His Lordship's wife goes missing, and a young woman is murdered and nobody is arrested, we draw the line. There is only so much wickedness we'll let Black Shuck get away with."

"Black Shuck is the devil's dog, and Sir Sandoe is the devil himself," added a large woman with a thin face and broad nose. She turned to face me. Her eyes narrowed. "Down from London, ain't ya? Well, someone's been doin' witchcraft and unleashed a curse on Bagington Hall. Ain't over yet, neither."

Hilda nodded and said, "Mark my words; this strike will grow like a snowball and be about as nasty as a Scottish winter."

There was a murmur of agreement, and we fell into a stilted silence.

Just then, I noticed George Edwards leaning against the stone wall, a little way off from the entrance. Besides the raised collars on his jacket, his body posture yielded nothing to the biting wind. In his hand, he carried a small brown paper bag from which he plucked a cobnut. He cracked the shell, popped the nut into his mouth, then became very still as if the temperature suddenly dropped below freezing and he'd turned into a block of ice.

"Like a cat watching a mouse," I muttered, following his gaze to the gatehouse.

A small man walking briskly waved at the gatekeeper. He wore a tweed jacket with matching trousers, a white shirt with heavy-starched collars, and a brown fedora hat. He walked with authoritative strides, head held high, despite the biting breeze.

"Sir Sandoe!"

It hadn't been yet a week since we'd met on the train to Cromer. I'd hope to dine with Lady Herriman and slip in and out of Bagington Hall unnoticed. His arrival complicated matters. I turned to look for Uncle Tristan. If he saw Sir Sandoe, he'd be sure to introduce me to the man, and then the game would be over. But Uncle was nowhere to be seen.

The large woman with the broad face and narrow nose whispered, "Look, it's Black Shuck himself on two legs!"

Sir Sandoe stood at the gate entrance, hands on hips, wide owl eyes taking in everything at once. Then his eyes settled on our small group of women, and in particular, me.

Oh bother!

Chapter 36

IN A MOVEMENT ALMOST too fast to follow, George Edwards spat the remains of his cobnut into the brown bag and scuttled over to Sir Sandoe, jabbed him on the shoulder and boomed, "I'm 'ere on behalf of Tommy."

Sir Sandoe turned his gaze from me to the man, a bemused expression on his face.

"Tommy who?"

"Crabapple," replied George in a soft voice. "The young fellow lost his feet working your land last harvest."

"Never heard of the lad."

George's mouth opened wide then closed. "But the boy almost died gathering the crops. You must remember him."

"Crabapple, you say? Ah, yes!" There was a trace of crimson around Sir Sandoe's peculiarly arched nostrils, and he stared at George Edwards with large, unblinking eyes. "Damn drunken fool."

George said, "Tommy doesn't drink, never has. His whole family are teatotallers."

Sir Sandoe's jaw tightened. His glance darted from George to the police officers, the gatekeeper and back again. He hesitated, clearly calculating his response.

"He'd been drinking brandy," he said sourly.

"You ordered your men to give it to him after the accident."

"Then the boy is an idiot," snapped Sir Sandoe. "Now what is it you want?"

George removed his cloth cap, gave a little bow, and said, "Sir, me name's George Edwards, with the agricultural union. But I'm 'ere today to speak with you man to man about compensation for Tommy. He can't work the land anymore."

"Come, come, man, he'll find another job."

"The boy ain't got no feet. Who would hire him?" There was a touch of frustration in George's voice.

Sir Sandoe placed a hand on his cheek as if in deep thought. A devious little smile touched the corners of his lips. "Well, I'd offer him a job in the house—"

"Very kind of you, sir," said George with another little bow. "I'll let the lad know at once."

Sir Sandoe's lips curved into a full-out grin, and he put on a mocking local accent. "But I don't trust nothin' with no feet." He let out a wild laugh, wiping a tear from his eye. "Now be off with you. We've had our fun."

George stood his ground. "The boy is living like a beast."

"Slithers about like a snake, does he?" Again, Sir Sandoe let out a laugh, this time doubling over. "I hear the circus is hiring."

"Sir, 'ave a little heart for the child. If it happened at the Blackwood Estate, they'd 'ave given 'im compensation."

Sir Sandoe's lips twisted into a snarl. "Compensation! He knew what he was getting into working the land. Everyone does. You get injured; that's your lookout."

This was too much for George. He grabbed Sir Sandoe by the collars, but the solid truncheon of Sergeant Pender knocked his rough hands away.

"Any more of this nonsense, and I'll have you arrested," said the sergeant.

George backed away.

At a safe distance, he raised his hand and pointed with a gnarled finger. "I'll not let you get away with treating the boy like that. The accident was on account of mechanical failure, not the boy's thoughtlessness."

A purple bloom crept slowly from Sir Sandoe's arched nostrils to cover his entire face. "As far as I'm concerned, old man, Tommy No-Feet can slither back to hell, and you with him."

"For the love o' God, sir," cried George. "Help the young boy to make a fresh start! He's... he's... been crippled working your land by your dangerous machines... Can't you see! You'll pay him compensation, or you'll regret it."

Sir Sandoe, mouth shut very tight, turned away. With quick, little steps high on the tips of his toes, he hurried through the gate, past the gatekeeper, and back into the extensive grounds of Bagington Hall.

Chapter 37

TEN MINUTES LATER, Uncle Tristan appeared hot and out of breath.

"Ladies, may I have your permission for my darling niece to take her leave, else she shall be late for an audience with Lady Herriman?"

Hilda said, "Rather you than me, dear. The old nag is as batty as a fruitcake steeped in rum."

The other women laughed in agreement.

"She's lonely," I said in her defence. "And from another era."

"Yeah, from ancient Rome," added the large woman with a broad face and narrow nose, "cos from what I hear, she works her house staff like slaves."

There was no laughter at this comment. It rang too true.

A few moments later, Uncle Tristan slid into the motorcar with a little smile on his lips. He glanced furtively over his shoulder. I followed his gaze towards a barren clump of hawthorn bushes. There was nothing to see, to the casual eye, and I wondered whether Lord Avalon, Man of Mystery, had spotted something I'd missed.

I said, "What are you looking at?"

"Lots of excitement about the place today," he replied, his voice as secretive as his glance.

There was something. I knew it, but what? And where had he been? I didn't see him in the gatehouse or amongst the men with the cloth caps. He'd simply vanished. But I knew better than to ask. If I were patient, he'd tell me soon enough.

"Anything exciting happen while you were waiting, Maggie?"

"Only Sir Sandoe," I replied in a casual voice. "His Lordship strolled to the gates to inspect things."

"What! Damn. I missed him." Uncle Tristan slapped his hand on the dashboard. Now I knew for sure that he wasn't in the gatehouse or with the men. So where was he? I waited, biding my time.

In a rather desperate voice, he said, "Did Sir Sandoe look like he was carrying my cheque?"

"Oh yes," I replied, having a little fun. "His Lordship carried it high in the air like some trophy from an ancient war."

"Maggie!"

"And George Edwards shook him about a little, but there was no sign of your bank cheque."

"What the blazes are you talking about?"

I told him about George Edwards' request for compensation for Tommy Crabapple and Sir Sandoe's response.

"My God! Why, Maggie, that's... that's absolutely depraved!"

Then I told him about the scuffle and finished with a word-for-word rendition of George Edwards' threat.

Uncle Tristan let it sink in. "Oooh. Big trouble is on the way. I can feel it. Discovery of gold or not, I'm not leaving this place without my cheque. From the grumblings I'm hearing, I wouldn't be surprised if the villagers show up en mass with pitchforks, blazing torches, and gasoline."

Unfortunately, I agreed. "That might be tonight!"

Uncle Tristan gave another furtive glance over his shoulder and started the engine.

"Better get a move on, then, else gruel will be back on the menu."

The motorcar eased forward. The circle of cloth-capped men parted. Sergeant Pender gave a salute; the gatekeeper waved us on, and we headed along the gravel road towards the carriage house.

Impatient to get to the bottom of where my uncle had been, I said, "With your powers of observation, you might have seen more than me when Sir Sandoe got into the scuffle, if you were here."

Uncle chuckled. "Lord Avalon, Man of Mystery, had other rather urgent business."

"Like what?"

"Frank Perry. I saw him skulking around by the stone wall, a short distance from where you and the ladies were talking."

"But I didn't see anyone!"

"Ah, that is because you were huddled together against the wind and facing the gatehouse. Almost missed the man, myself. Frank was crouched low against a hawthorn bush. He took off when he saw me, and I give chase. Nearly ran over Vicar Humberstone."

"What on earth was he doing?"

"By the looks of it, hunting. He had a bow and quiver of arrows slung across his shoulder. The man better take care. I hear there are rabid foxes in these parts. Strange behaviour for a man of the cloth, if you ask me."

"Not the vicar! What was Frank Perry doing?"

Uncle Tristan did not speak for a moment. When he did, it was in a soft whisper. "Maggie, I simply wanted to return his envelope.

You should have seen the look on his face when I whipped it out of my cape."

Chapter 38

I KNEW SOMETHING WAS wrong when Withers showed up.

Uncle Tristan and Boots left to search for Sir Sandoe while I waited for the head butler. Withers arrived moments after they left, his tall, dapper figure moving with the grace of a cat. He ambled along the path, swinging his Victorian sword cane about as if he were the lord of the manor.

To my astonishment, he wore a finely tailored tweed jacket with matching trousers, a white shirt with heavily starched collars, and a brown fedora hat—an almost identical replica of Sir Sandoe's attire. And a better-looking one at that!

I gazed at the man with undisguised surprise. "Withers?"

He gave his distinctive little bow. It was him, all right, but the attire was not what one expects from a butler nor was his language.

"Ah, Miss Darling. Terrible weather we're having. The newspaper says it is just for a day or so, and then we'll be back to the unusually warm sunshine. Now, you are here for an audience with Louisa?"

"Louisa?"

"Lady Herriman, to you."

This was highly unusual; servants were never on first-name terms with their employers. It was a rule adhered to in the solid

Edwardian mansions of London and the rural Victorian manors of Norfolk. For a moment, my heart froze. Had Uncle Tristan's prediction of villages overthrowing the landlord come true?

I gazed about the place looking for signs of an angry mob with pitchforks and blazing torches. But everything appeared to be in order. I mentally sorted through all the other possibilities and drew a blank.

Perplexed, I said, "What happened to your uniform, the one with the big buttons and white gloves?"

Withers said, "The black tailcoat, shirt, and waistcoat were appropriate attire as the head butler. Lady Herriman has promoted me to head of the estate. My new position requires the dress and conversational poise of a gentleman."

I did not fully grasp the meaning of Withers' words, for a moment, then my mouth formed an O as my eyes widened. "Isn't that Sir Sandoe's responsibility?"

Withers' voice went quiet. "Things have changed now the air has been cleared."

I wasn't sure what he meant but took a chance and said, "Since the funeral of Miss Antoinette?"

"A lovely child but too inquisitive for her own good." Withers shut his eyes. I wondered what the butler saw under those closed lids. When his eyes reopened, they glistened, and he spoke as if to himself. "Sir Sandoe is a heavy burden. It is my duty to relieve Lady Herriman of the load."

I was still thinking about his words when I remembered his conversation with Vicar Humberstone. Withers had the old chambermaid's room sealed off. But that would have been under orders. The question that ran through my mind was who gave the order?

My heart beat a mile a minute as I said, "Withers, did Sir Sandoe instruct you to seal off the old chambermaid's quarters?"

Withers clasped his fingers tight about the sword cane and un-
clasped them again. "Miss Darling, we shall have no more talk on
this issue."

My eyebrows rose and fell. "Withers, answer the—"

He raised a hand. "It is Mr Withers or sir, to you, from now on.
Is that clear?"

I stood and stared at the man for a long moment. His hooded
eyes stared back. They flashed with an undertone of the rage he'd
unleashed on Mrs Mullins during my first visit.

"Never bring this matter up again." Withers punctuated each
word with the sword cane as he spoke. "Erase it from your memory,
and let it be."

When I was younger, I would have backed down, but working
in a pie-and-mash shop had removed my fear of difficult people.
They were commonplace in London. I had to be careful though. If
I pushed him too hard, he might persuade Her Ladyship to cancel
Tristan's Hands' contract, or worse, strike out at me with his Victo-
rian sword cane.

I weighed it all up, took a deep breath, and said, "Mr Withers,
do you know who killed Miss Antoinette?"

"What did I just say?"

But I couldn't let Miss Antoinette's murder rest. "As the head
butler, you must have seen or heard something. What did you see?"

Withers raised a hand, palm out. "Chief Inspector Little has
closed the investigation."

"You didn't answer my question."

"Nosing about will get you into trouble, might even cost you
your contract with Bagington Hall."

I ignored the threat. "Did you give a statement to the chief inspector?"

He eyed me as a robin does an undersized worm. "One of your first tasks is to find a replacement head butler. Lady Herriman shall discuss the details with you over dinner. But I insist on having the final word, is that clear?"

My eyes blinked rapidly. "Y-Y-Yes," I said. "But can you tell me what you know about the death of Miss Antoinette?"

Withers sighed loudly then ran a finger over his hairline moustache. "Please come with me to the scullery where I shall leave you in the capable hands of Mrs Mullins."

Uncle had been right, I thought, as I followed a step behind with more questions than answers. Big trouble was brewing at Bagington Hall, and it wasn't just to do with the agricultural strike.

Chapter 39

WHEN WITHERS LEFT, Mrs Mullins motioned me to join her at the table.

I wasn't sure where her niece was, but she wasn't in the scullery, and that was good because there were a hundred questions I wanted to ask before Dolly Trimmings or anyone else showed up.

Mrs Mullins reached into a handbag and pulled out an oversized silver flask and took a swig. The air soured with the smell of cheap brandy.

"Miss Darling, I was just taking a break from me duties. The brandy's medicinal on account of my weak heart, doctor's orders. Nice to sit 'ere, look through the scullery windows, and enjoy a little peace, don't ya think?"

I nodded, and we sat in silence for a moment staring out the large windows which looked out onto a small yard and brick wall. I would be patient. Sometimes it paid off; sometimes it did not, but I had to know more about what was going on in Bagington Hall.

After she had taken another swig, I said, "I see Withers has received a promotion."

"Don't call him that no more. It is 'sir' now, or if you want to get on his good side, call 'im, 'me lord.' Anything else, and the man explodes in a rage."

I'd seen Withers' vicious temper and knew he was equally spiteful with animals. I remembered the look of disappointment on his face when I insisted on taking Swiftee away from this place. And then there was the string noose and a knife he carried in his jacket pocket. Today he'd tolerated my questions. With his new elevated position, I knew that wouldn't last long.

I said, "What on earth is going on at Bagington Hall?"

"Ain't for me to say. I just work 'ere to help pay my way. I'm a widow, you know. This 'ere job is all I got, and gossiping don't do me no good."

I tried a different tactic. "Swiftee is doing well in his new home. And he is growing fat."

A glimmer of a smile touched the corner of her lips. "I'll 'ave to tell our Rose about that."

"Let her know he caught a mouse."

"Was it three-legged?"

We both laughed.

I said, "Rose can visit whenever she is free. Swiftee would like to see her."

Mrs Mullins visibly relaxed. "Would you like a slice of seed cake?"

I nodded.

She stood up, hurried to a cupboard, and came back with two plates.

As I tucked in, I knew time was running out. I wanted answers before Dolly Trimmings showed up to whisk me away to meet with Lady Herriman.

In the pie-and-mash shop, we often gave away free samples. On those days, we sold out. I tried something similar in the hopes it would open Mrs Mullins' lips.

"Tristan's Hands are looking for staff," I said in a low voice. "Can I add you to our household list?"

"Don't Mr Harbottle rent that tiny loft above John and Sons butcher shop?"

"It is a temporary location."

Mrs Mullins scowled. "They say Bagington Hall is Mr Harbottle's only account, and I work here as it is."

"There will be other accounts."

"When?"

I changed tack. "Maybe you ought to just tell me what is on your mind."

Mrs Mullins took a bite of seed cake. After chewing, she said, "Withers has Sir Sandoe and everyone else under his thumb. You'll be next; mark my words."

I leaned across the table, placed a hand on hers. "I'm listening. What do you know?"

Mrs Mullins opened her mouth to speak then closed it, withdrew her hands, picked up the plates, and walked over to the kitchen sink. There she washed up and placed the items on a wooden draining rack.

When Mrs Mullins was finished, she turned and said, "Miss Darling, I'm sorry, but I don't think it would be wise to discuss such things, especially with me being a widow and very much in need of this position."

I was about to give up when a different question popped into my mind.

"Tell me about Miss Antoinette?"

"Now there is another story. Miss Antoinette was such a lovely girl, and she stood up for the servants..." Her voice trailed off.

We sat in silence. After what must have been a minute, I said, "Well?"

Mrs Mullins looked around the small scullery as if someone might be hiding in a corner and listening to us. "Since you found her body, I don't suppose it will do no harm for you to know."

"I'm listening. Start at the beginning and go right through to the end."

The sound of footsteps came from the hall.

Mrs Mullins lifted her eyes to mine. "Keep this to yourself."

The footsteps grew louder. I willed her to hurry but kept my mouth shut.

Mrs Mullins looked at her hands. "Miss Antoinette planned to run away. She was sweet on a young gentleman. I know because I helped set up their clandestine meetings. They planned to wed and leave for America. Once they'd settled down, she promised to send for me. But Sir Sandoe found out. I wouldn't have gone anyway."

This time I said nothing. All I could do was listen.

Mrs Mullins let out a long sigh. "There is always trouble when a woman wants to marry below her station in life. Miss Antoinette was keen on a union lad not from around these parts. A young fellow by the name of Frank Perry."

Chapter 40

"MISS DARLING, IS IT you?"

Dolly Trimmings stood in the entrance of the scullery. Her wide hippopotamus mouth hung slightly open, and she panted like a mountain pack mule at the end of a steep climb.

"Oh, Gawd, yes, yes, you are here!"

She wore an elaborate mauve gown with gold stars and a little, matching bonnet pinned to her blonde hair. It perched like a sparrow's nest on her round, plump face from which her birdlike eyes twitched around the scullery. A necklace of huge pearls hung from her neck, and in her hand, she carried a large goblet.

"Oh Lordy, Miss Darling, I'm so pleased you are here." Dolly hurried to the kitchen table, put down the goblet, and threw her arms about me. There was a strong pong of plum wine about her person.

"Lady Herriman has been like a sour toad all day. I knows when she sees you, she'll cheer up. You keeps her gabbing, so she don't get to thinking about how miserable Sir Sandoe makes her life. You 'ave a magic touch with getting people to talk."

Indeed I do, I thought. And if you'd given me another ten minutes with Mrs Mullins, I'd have the answers to my questions.

I wanted to know more about Miss Antoinette's relationship with Frank Perry and Sir Sandoe's reaction.

But Dolly's arrival had put an end to my enquiries. It was time for dinner with Lady Herriman, and that, I feared, was to be endured rather than enjoyed. The nauseating thought of roast swan with buttered potatoes left me feeling as vinegary as a caged crab. I wondered whether we'd start with calf's head soup and refused to think about what awaited for dessert.

I glanced at Mrs Mullins. She sat, arms folded, a cold expression on her face. I itched to finish our conversation. How had Sir Sandoe discovered the relationship between Miss Antoinette and Frank Perry? What had the man done about it? Did he order Withers to shutter the old chambermaid's room? What happened to Lady Sandoe? And who did Mrs Mullins think murdered Miss Antoinette?

Answers to those questions would have to wait. I said, "Mrs Mullins, shall we talk later?"

"No," she replied with a firm shake of her head. "I've spoken out of turn. There is nothing more I will say on the matter."

Dolly glared at Mrs Mullins. "Now just what 'ave you be saying to Miss Darling?"

Mrs Mullins met her gaze with a defiant look. "None of your business."

"If it is to do with Bagington Hall, it is my business," Dolly snapped. "Things are changing around here, and I have the ear of Her Ladyship."

"One of these days," began Mrs Mullins in a threatening tone, "Her Ladyship will find out you've been wearing her clothes and drinking her wine, and then you'll be done for."

"Keep your mouth shut and eyes closed. Now what were you telling Miss Darling about our dearly departed Miss Antoinette?"

Mrs Mullins said, "How would you know what we was talking about unless you was snooping?"

"How dare you!" Dolly shrilled.

Mrs Mullins placed her hands on the arms of her chair. I thought she would get up, but after a brief hesitation, she only said, "Me and Miss Darling was talking private business."

Dolly turned to face me. "Miss Darling, you shall tell me everything when we are in Lady Herriman's waiting chamber."

I cleared my throat. "I gave my word to keep Mrs Mullins' confidence."

Mrs Mullins added, "Like I say, it ain't none of your business."

"Suit yourself," replied Dolly, her eyes blazing. "When I tell Withers, he'll get it out of you."

"Black Shuck himself couldn't get a peep from me lips," said Mrs Mullins, standing up. "Now, if you don't mind, I've got work to do." She walked to the kitchen sink, picked up the plates from the wooden draining rack, wiped them with a dishcloth, and idly gazed through the window.

A moment later, Mrs Mullins clutched at her chest, tilted her head back, and let out an ear-piercing scream.

Chapter 41

EVERYTHING SLOWED FOR a terrible moment.

Mrs Mullins let out another chilling shriek and collapsed against the sink, her top half tipping into the large iron bowl. Bewildered, I clambered to my feet, stumbled forward, sucking in air, heart pounding like a tin drum against my chest.

Before I reached the sink, Dolly yelled, "Heart attack. Mrs Mullins has a weak chest. She's dead!"

I kept moving forward.

"Oh my God," yelled Dolly. "Doctor! We need to telephone for Dr Swensen!"

But we did not need to make the call.

At the sink, I placed an arm around Mrs Mullins' shoulder. Her head reared up, eyes wide open. Again, she let out a terrifying screech, her entire body shuddering as if bitten by a rabid fox.

Confused and alarmed, I stepped back fearful Mrs Mullins would soon start foaming at the mouth. But there was no madness in her eyes or uncontrollable twitching of her limbs, only a look of savage fear.

"Mrs Mullins," I cried. "Is it your heart?"

In astonishment, I watched as she raised her arm. It moved very slowly as if the muscles were filled with rusted iron. The index finger unfurled from a trembling hand to point to the scullery window.

I stood there staring, breath ragged as my mind tried to make sense of the image sent to it by my eyes.

"Dear God!"

Slumped against the dingy brick wall, a figure lay motionless. My stomach roiled when I spotted the growing pool of blood glisten in the fading evening light.

For some seconds, I could neither think nor scream as my eyes took it all in: the tweed jacket, brown fedora at a rakish angle, the polished shoes, and the silver envelope clutched tight in the right fist.

Dolly was at the sink now. She stared in disbelief at the gruesome scene.

"Sir Sandoe!" she shrieked. "Dr Swensen! We must telephone for help."

But there was no need to call for a doctor.

Sir Richard Sandoe was definitely dead.

That realisation hit like a blow to the solar plexus, forcing me to gasp for air.

"Dear God!" cried Mrs Mullins. "Black Shuck is upon us again!"

A low black shape appeared from the shadows.

Mrs Mullins let loose another terrified scream. "The beast himself!"

But it wasn't a dog. It was a man!

And he wore heavy black boots; shabby, grey, flannel trousers; a jacket patched at the elbows; and a flat cloth cap. I recognised him instantly—Frank Perry.

He held a bloodied dagger in his left hand and remained low to the ground as if he were afraid to move.

When Mrs Mullins let out another scream, he forced himself upright and turned to the window. His eyes caught mine for a brief second. There was confusion, fear, and blind panic in the orbs.

At that moment, Withers, Boots, and Uncle Tristan arrived.

Frank backed up a few steps, shock and fear etched into his face.

"You'll swing for this," said Withers. "Now put your hands in the air, and don't give us any reason to harm you."

For a moment, Frank stood stock-still, his eyes staring at the body. He dropped the dagger. It clattered to the ground with a metallic thud.

"That's it," said Withers, pulling a knife from his pocket. "Hands up high where we can see them."

Frank turned, and with the agility of an acrobat, scrambled over the wall.

Within minutes, men were shouting all over the place. Police whistles blasted. Confusion was everywhere. The entire staff of Bagington Hall were running here and there searching for Frank Perry as the evening light faded to dark.

Chapter 42

"IT'S LADY HERRIMAN I feel sorry for," said Chief Inspector Little with a shake of his head. "Her Ladyship took the news well but now has to run Bagington Hall alone, and at her age!"

The chief inspector stood by the open door of the scullery eyeing Sergeant Pender, who sat at the kitchen table nursing a mug of "fortified" tea. Dolly and Mrs Mullins and I were the other occupants, each with our own mug: Withers, Boots, and Uncle Tristan having joined the manhunt for Frank Perry.

"Mrs Mullins," said the chief inspector, "I believe you found the body?"

"Yes, sir," began Mrs Mullins with a hesitant voice. "Sir Sandoe was slumped against the wall all owl like."

"Owl like?" Chief Inspector Little pulled out a sheet of paper from his top pocket and a pen from a side pocket.

"Arms spread like wings and eyes wide open as"—Mrs Mullins took a sip from her mug and relaxed a little—"if he'd been taken by surprise."

"Ah, please go on."

Mrs Mullins needed no further encouragement. "And his mouth was twisted as if his life were flashing before 'im, showing 'im all the evil deeds he'd done." She was in her element, rehearsing the story she'd repeat to the eager villagers. "So twisted even his own mother wouldn't recognize him. So twisted it were like—"

"Yes, yes. I get the picture," interrupted the chief inspector. "Is there anything else?"

"It were terrible," replied Mrs Mullins. "What with the wide eyes, twisted mouth, and all that blood, I knew he was done in."

The chief inspector shuddered then said, "And what about you, Miss Trimmings? Do you have anything to add to what Mrs Mullins has said?"

"No, sir. I ain't got no more to say, other than I hope you catch Mr Frank Perry real quick, cos a man like that is like a viper. He'll strike again."

The chief inspector's head moved up and down with vigour. "Criminals like to return to the scene of their crime to gloat. Sergeant Pender, set up patrols day and night around Bagington Hall."

"Righto, sir."

"And you, Miss Darling," said the chief inspector, "anything you'd like to add?"

I placed my hands around the mug and gazed towards the window. I could hear muffled voices from outside, a constant reminder of the troubling events of the evening.

There were several things that concerned me. How did Frank get so close to the main house without being spotted? Why would he attack Sir Sandoe at Bagington Hall where the chances of being caught were so high? Frank Perry didn't strike me as irrational and crazed, but maybe I was wrong on that one.

But what puzzled me most was Sir Richard Sandoe. His little hand had grasped tight on to an envelope, and one I recognised.

It was the letter Uncle Tristan had returned to Frank Perry. Now I wanted to know its contents.

"There was a silver envelope in Sir Sandoe's hand," I said. "I suppose you have opened and read it?"

Chief Inspector Little turned to Sergeant Pender. "Did you open the envelope; what was inside?"

The sergeant took a gulp from his mug then stood up and hurried to the sink where he tapped on the window.

"Constable Lutz, do you have the envelope?"

The reply came back muffled but audible.

"What envelope, sir?"

"A silver one, in Sir Sandoe's hand."

"No, sir. There wasn't any envelope with the body."

"Did you look under the body?"

"No, sir."

"Then move it and look."

"Are you sure we shouldn't wait for Dr Swensen, sir?"

"Move the body, Constable."

There were several large grunts, followed by a startled, dry-throated cry.

"No, sir," came the shaky voice of Constable Lutz. "No envelope under the body."

"Perhaps he should check the pockets," I said.

"Check the pockets," boomed the sergeant.

"Is that necessary, sir?"

"Lutz, check the pockets."

We waited in silence. I closed my eyes for several seconds, my mind racing over the events of the evening. Yes, the envelope was in Sir Sandoe's right hand. There was no doubt about it.

At last, Constable Lutz spoke, his voice thin and trembling.

"All his pockets are empty, sir. No envelope, not even a pocket watch or a coin."

"But I saw it in his hand," I protested.

Chief Inspector Little said, "Mrs Mullins, did you see an envelope?"

She shook her head. "I wasn't looking for no envelope. Seeing a dead body was enough for me. I wasn't looking for that neither. But I saw it all right."

The chief inspector said, "What about you, Miss Trimmings?"

"Lots of blood," cried Dolly. "And that monster with the dagger. I saw all that for a fact, but I didn't see any silver envelope."

Idly, the chief inspector slipped the pen back into his jacket pocket. With one hand, he folded the sheet of paper then folded it again.

"Miss Darling, shock does terrible things to the unprepared mind. The letter was nothing but a figment of your gaudy, female imagination."

I stared at him, anger thick at the back of my throat. "Chief Inspector, I know what I saw."

"Now, now, dear woman, don't let your emotions get carried away. There was no envelope. Let that be the end of the matter. I suggest you take a nice long sip from that lovely mug of tea, and you'll feel much better."

Fighting back anger, I cleared my throat and said, "There was a silver envelope in his right fist. I am certain of what I—"

"I am afraid," interrupted the chief inspector, "I cannot spend precious police time chasing phantoms concocted from the feminine mind. The unfortunate death of Sir Sandoe is an all-too-common case of assault and robbery gone wrong. That his pockets are empty confirms my suspicion. Now where the devil is Frank Perry?"

Chapter 43

"FRANK SEEMED LIKE SUCH a nice lad," said Mrs Mullins.

"He's the dark brooding type," replied Sergeant Pender. "Never know what they are thinking. I knew he was one to keep an eye on, and I was right!" He turned to the chief inspector. "The lad got into a scuffle with the gatekeeper."

"Ah," Chief Inspector Little said, leaning forward. "Please tell me more."

The sergeant put on an official tone. "On Monday, the first day of the agricultural strike, Mr Perry tried to sneak into Bagington Hall on the back of a delivery van. The gatehouse keeper spotted him, and there was a violent scuffle."

"Point?" Chief Inspector Little said.

"Mr Perry claimed to have a letter for Sir Sandoe."

"Letter?" The chief inspector's eyes fastened on mine. "In a silver envelope, by any chance?"

Sergeant Pender's lips curved into a faint smile. "When I searched him, there was no letter. But he was carrying somethin' silver—a long-handled dagger."

Chief Inspector Little walked to the sink, stared through the window.

"I noticed a dagger by the body, Sergeant."

176

"Indeed, sir."

"Do you recognise it?"

"The very same weapon I found in Frank Perry's possession, sir."

The chief inspector sucked in a breath. "Mr Perry will swing before the year is out. Now write up the report, and have it on my desk by noon tomorrow. Add Dr Swensen's comments when you get them."

"Aye, sir." Sergeant Pender took a long sip from his mug. "The thing is, sir, Frank Perry might not have worked alone."

"Go on."

"Frank was with the agricultural union. He came to Norfolk with George Edwards."

"The national union organiser?"

"That'd be him."

"Point?"

"George Edwards threatened Sir Sandoe at the gatehouse earlier today."

"Coincidence?"

"That's what I thought, but you see, a young lad by the name of Tommy Crabapple—"

"I know the story, Sergeant. A terrible accident, wrote the report up myself. The whole incident shook up Sir Sandoe, I can tell you. Not good when workers drink on duty, not good at all."

"Aye, sir." Sergeant Pender placed both hands over his mug. "But George Edwards claimed the accident was a result of mechanical failure. He said Tommy Crabapple was teatotaller and was drunk because—"

"That's quite enough! I got the facts from Sir Sandoe himself." Chief Inspector Little closed his eyes and was silent for a long moment. "And you say George Edwards and Frank Perry are acquaintances?"

"Aye, sir."

"I suppose it'd take someone as crafty as Mr Edwards to help Frank." Chief Inspector Little nodded to the window. "How else could he have got so far without being seen?"

"And Frank's long-handled dagger, sir," added Sergeant Pender. "It is the same type Dr Swensen found plunged deep into the chest of Miss Antoinette."

Again, the chief inspector sucked in a sharp breath. "My God, man, we'd better tread carefully with this one."

"Shall I bring Mr Edwards in for questioning, sir?"

"Good God, no! Agricultural workers from all over England would flood here in protest... and Scotland Yard might get involved. No, Norfolk's in enough chaos as it is. There has to be an alternative explanation."

"But what, sir?" Sergeant Pender took another sip from his mug.

"Leave it with me, Sergeant. I'll work everything out. You concentrate on the report and finding Frank Perry. The sooner he swings, the better."

Chapter 44

EARLY SATURDAY AFTERNOON, I sat at my desk in Uncle Tristan's loft office practising calligraphy. There was little activity in the curing yard. The stagnant, musty odour of the place was less intense than a weekday. Twenty-four hours hadn't yet passed since the death of Sir Sandoe, and Frank Perry was still on the run.

For the third or fourth time, I'd pressed too hard on the acute accent over the Gaelic vowels.

"Oh bother!"

Uncle tilted back in his chair, feet propped up on his desk with his hands behind his head. "Maggie, you should show your penmanship. Your characters are well drawn; it could open up another career."

I shook my head and smiled. "It's a hobby, one I enjoy. I'm not sure it would be so much fun if I did it for a living."

The focused concentration and subtle hand movements of calligraphy were more of a therapy against the flotsam and jetsam of everyday life. But today it wasn't working. I put the pencil down.

Uncle stared off into space. "Ah, well," he said forlornly, "what are we doing here on this fine last Saturday of the month?"

"Keeping away from the gossips." A hunger pang stabbed at my stomach. I'd missed breakfast at Mrs Rusbridger's boarding house to avoid everyone. Too many questions. And there was something else. The guests had begun to regard me with a wary eye.

There was a sudden intensity to the foul air. I gasped and wondered who in their right mind would willingly visit this dim, pungent place.

Uncle Tristan read my thoughts and said in a gloomy voice, "I can't see the likes of Lady Herriman climbing the stairs of a butcher shop to book our business."

"It takes time for the word to spread," I said.

But Uncle Tristan was in a glum mood. "Nobody has signed up. Not a cook, footman, or even a yard hand."

"A little patience is all that is required."

"Patience!" cried Uncle Tristan, tapping his feet on his desk. "Our office stinks like the devil's breath. We are a staffing agency with no staff. It's as if there is some... some blasted curse hovering over the business. Even the man who gave me the idea is dead!" He frowned. "Oh, Maggie, your father is the one with the business brains. Was the staffing agency a terrible mistake?"

Now wasn't the time to mention that Father's business ventures weren't glittering successes. Everything he'd turned his hand to in London had met with difficulty: the fish shop on Seven Sisters Road closed, and his venture into the horse-drawn cab trade ended in failure. Father's only stable employment was as an assistant in a bakery shop.

"Come now, Uncle, cheer up. Sir Sandoe's murder has nothing to do with Tristan's Hands. And this office is temporary until things right themselves. Look on the bright side: we have one client."

His frown deepened into a scowl. "You know what Lady Herriman thinks about me."

"The woman is just out of touch, and now she has to take on the burden of running Bagington Hall. Can't you offer her a little kindness in her period of mourning?"

But Uncle Tristan continued in his downbeat tone. "With Sir Sandoe gone, the sour, old toad will cancel our contract. I can feel it in my bones."

I picked up the pencil. "Oh, don't be so pessimistic, Bagington Hall is the first client of many; you said as much yourself."

Uncle Tristan let out a long, low sigh. "Better than the bakery business, that's what I told him. Why did I not wait for confirmation?"

I put the pencil down. "What are you talking about?"

"Your father, Maggie. I told him about the gold mine in Peru." There was a raspy tremble to his voice.

"Yes, I know," I said, trying to quiet my own rising sense of unease. "You said you were going to write."

"To give him an update on his investments." Uncle Tristan's face twisted into a wild, almost hysterical look. "Your father has already joined me in the venture. He has invested all his savings."

"Dear God!" A sour sensation filled my stomach. I turned away to stare at the wall in front of my desk. "Everything?"

"And the money he put aside for you to care for your sister, Nancy, after his death."

I turned back to Uncle Tristan, dismayed.

"But what if..." I paused. There was little to be gained by panic. It only clouded the mind and left one feeling helpless. The money had been invested, and there was nothing that could be done about that. And the gold? I didn't know what to think. I said, "You must visit with Lady Herriman and return with the bank cheque."

"On Monday," replied Uncle Tristan. "Any sooner would appear disrespectful to the memory of Sir Sandoe."

"Indeed," I said, already feeling a little less panicked. "Her Ladyship will be in deep mourning after the events of the week. Nevertheless, it would be wise to get the bank cheque and cash it with all haste."

Chapter 45

WE SAT IN SILENCE IN the tiny office on the top floor of John and Sons butcher shop. Occasionally, Uncle Tristan let out a sigh, or the stench-ridden air would intensify, and we'd both begin a bout of coughing.

It was going to be a long wait until Monday morning. I intended to travel with him to Bagington Hall. While he met with Lady Herriman, I'd do a little snooping, see what I could find out about the death of Miss Antoinette, and pick up any titbits on the police investigation into Sir Sandoe's murder.

"I'd feel a lot better," began Uncle Tristan, after a particularly heavy sigh, "if I'd have got the bank cheque yesterday even if I had to pick-pocket it from Sir Sandoe's corpse." He paused, eyes darting towards the door. Then he lowered his voice. "If Withers and Boots weren't with me, I'd have checked his pockets."

"Ah-ha!" I stood to my feet. "The great Lord Avalon, Man of Mystery, strikes again!"

"Eh?"

"You took the envelope. How on earth did you manage it?"

"Maggie, what are you talking about?"

"The silver envelope, Uncle. The one you gave to Frank Perry. It was in Sir Sandoe's fist when I saw the body."

Uncle Tristan closed his eyes and became very still. Under the closed lids his eyeballs moved in little darting motions. It was as if they were putting together fragments of a filed-away memory.

When his lids lifted, he said, "Yes, I saw it also. It was in his right hand. Are you saying it vanished?"

"It wasn't with his body when the police arrived."

Uncle shook his head. "Maggie, I didn't take it nor did Frank Perry. I had the man in my sights the entire time."

I met Uncle Tristan's gaze. The room was silent around us, the lack of weekday clatter and clangs intensifying the stillness.

I sat down, picked up my pencil, chewed the end, and thought for a moment. Speaking slowly, I said, "It must have been taken by Boots or Withers."

"Or someone else. There was a lot of activity around the body."

That was true. Anyone might have snatched it. The only fact was that the silver envelope was in Sir Sandoe's right hand, and now it was gone. Who took the envelope, and why?

Uncle Tristan placed a hand over his eyes. "Whoever swiped the envelope is sharper than me. Why didn't I think to search Sir Sandoe's pockets for my bank cheque?"

"You needn't have bothered," I said. "His pockets were empty."

Uncle Tristan's eyebrows shot up. "Did you search him?"

"Constable Lutz did. Nothing. Not even a scrap of paper or a coin. The officer even looked under the body."

"But he must have had my cheque about him." He looked up, his face set as if a new revelation about the character of Sir Sandoe had just hit him. "The man gave me his word!"

"Maybe he left it on his writing desk... or perhaps Frank Perry rifled through his pockets and took what he could before we spotted him."

Uncle Tristan stared off into the distance. "Frank didn't take it. What would he do with a bank cheque? He could hardly cash it."

"Maybe on the black market."

"Frank is not some underworld man of crime."

"He's wanted for the murder of Sir Richard Sandoe, and they might even link him to the death of Miss Antoinette."

"Stuff and nonsense! Frank Perry didn't murder Sir Sandoe, and as for Miss Antoinette, well, she was the last person he'd harm."

A certainty in my uncle's tone caused me to pause. I thought about the brief glance of Frank through the scullery window and felt deep down he was as startled as myself to see the body. But, then again, he had a dagger in his hand, the one used to murder Sir Sandoe.

"Guilty or innocent," I said, "it doesn't look particularly good for him."

"That's why I agreed to—"

A sharp, hard knock on the door interrupted our conversation.

"Come in," shouted Uncle Tristan.

The door latch raised. It swung open with a sharp creak.

The long swan neck of Boots peered around the door, his narrow, bloodshot eyes like slits of glitter in the gloom. He hesitated.

"Enter," boomed Uncle Tristan.

Boots stepped into the room. He wore polished, black shoes, a neatly pressed chauffeur suit, white shirt with stiff collars, and on his head, a peaked cap. His eyes darted about as if he were afraid a fiend might jump out of the shadows.

"Phew, it stinks worse than the devil's cesspit in 'ere. How can yer stand it?"

Uncle Tristan ignored the comment, stood to his feet, and said, "To what do we owe this pleasure?"

"Mrs Rusbridger mentioned Miss Darling would be 'ere."

Uncle Tristan frowned. "Did Lady Herriman send you?"

"Aye, and I've been driving all over. Just come from the boarding 'ouse. The ladies were all agitated about the events of last night, an' said you'd be at the butcher shop. I come straight over."

Uncle said, "Has something happened to Withers?"

"Mr Withers ain't doing no more driving about the place. Now I'm the chauffeur, footman, and anything else." Boots grimaced then spoke with the dry hiss of a snake. "I'm at his beck and call worse than a hound dog. More work, same pay. It ain't bloody right!"

"Would you like to join us?" said Uncle Tristan, his voice fast and eager. "I'll add your name to our new staffing agency."

Boots froze on the spot, blanching.

"Well... I... er... you see—"

"Come, come, man. You can be our very first worker. Now what do you say?"

"No, no, no. I can't be doing no deals with the"—his voice dropped off, and he began to tremble—"like that. So I thank yer very much, but no thank you."

Uncle Tristan winced. "Well, what do you want of Miss Darling?"

Boots turned to me and gave a low bow. "Lady Herriman sends 'er apologies for the cancelled dinner yesterday evening and requests yer attendance for an evening audience."

"When?" Uncle Tristan and I said simultaneously.

Boots pulled out a gold pocket watch and scrutinised it for several seconds.

"Dinner will be served in about an hour and a half. They have sent me to drive you over."

"Thank God!" cried Uncle Tristan, jumping to his feet and prancing over to where I sat. He grabbed hold of my shoulders so fiercely I almost cried out. "Maggie, ask her about the gold, my bank cheque, your advance, and when we can expect payment for our services."

"We must leave now, else we will be late," said Boots. "And Her Ladyship is in a sour enough mood as it is."

I stood up and followed Boots through the door. Uncle Tristan hurried behind.

"Bring home the bacon, Maggie. Your ole uncle, father, and sister, Nancy, are counting on you."

Chapter 46

IT WAS A DULL AND CHEERLESS afternoon with the sun hidden behind a bank of dark clouds. Boots eased the motorcar onto the narrow lane, his white-gloved hands on the steering wheel. Every now and then, he'd take his eyes from the road to peer into the back as if I might be a dangerous snake.

I said, "Boots, did you happen to see a silver envelope near Sir Sandoe's body yesterday evening?"

His head swivelled and fixed me with a direct gaze. "Don't like to remember it, Miss Darling."

"Now think, close your eyes... no, don't do that, but did you perhaps pick up the envelope?"

"It were a right bloody awful sight. Like a scene from hell. Not the sort o' thing a lady ought to think about neither."

I ignored the rebuke and persisted. "Or perhaps you saw someone else pick it up?"

Boots turned back to the road. "Like I says, that's not what an honest, God-fearing man puts his mind to." He raised a white-gloved hand from the steering wheel. "Her Ladyship 'as asked that I walk you to her private chambers."

The finality to his tone made it clear there would be no answer to my question.

I loathed the thought of being at the beck and call of Lady Herriman. But until Tristan's Hands had additional clients, there was little I could do about the situation. And then there was the problem of staff. So far, no one had signed up for the agency. Not even Mrs Mullins, who I witnessed being abused by Withers; nor Boots, who had been ordered to work for less pay.

"Until we get new clients and staff sign-ups," I muttered, "all we've got is a stench-filled room at the top of a butcher shop and no money."

Boots' long neck twisted at the sound of my voice, his eyes making contact with mine for an instant before he turned back to look at the road.

Suddenly my mouth went dry, and I was swept up by a violent desire to tell Her Ladyship where she could shove our contract. The thought caused me to laugh out loud.

"Ha-ha-ha-ha."

It sounded like the cackle of a witch.

Boots slowed the vehicle to a crawl, his eyes peering into the back of the motorcar. Again, our eyes met, then he turned around, and the motorcar picked up speed.

A renewed wave of determination washed over me. I'd ask Lady Herriman directly about the gold mines, Uncle Tristan's bank cheque, advance payment for Tristan's Hands services, and demand Withers tell me everything he knew about the death of Miss Antoinette.

I swallowed hard at the memory of her desiccated body and breathed in deeply to control a rising anger at the lack of progress by the local constabulary.

"I will be persistent and polite. But I have to get answers."

For the fourth or fifth time, Boots twisted his head to peer into the rear. The motorcar swerved, narrowly missing the hedge that ran alongside the lane.

"Keep your eyes on the road," I yelled. "Else you'll have us both mangled and dead in a ditch with Black Shuck gnawing on our bones!"

His dry, raspy gulp was audible.

"Beggin' yer pardon, miss."

But a minute later, his head rotated, beady eyes peering into the back.

Annoyed, I said, "Have you been to the Norwich zoo lately?"

"No, miss."

"Is that why you are watching me like some exotic exhibit?"

His long neck flushed. "I don't wish to appear rude, miss."

"Really!" I let the word hang in the air. "Then why are you staring?"

A tide of crimson washed up his neck to his face. Again, he turned. His beady eyes met mine. The whites were reddish, and he looked fearful. Or tired. Or both.

"Everyone at Bagington Hall is talking, miss. Not me, mind you. I ain't got no time for gossip and don't spread it neither."

But I could tell in the anxious line of his jaw, the half-furtive look in the eye, there was something gnawing at him. All that he needed was a little prod, and his lips would begin to flap.

I said, "I suppose the talk at Bagington Hall is all about the murder of Sir Sandoe."

"Yes, miss, and Miss Antoinette"—his voice darkened—"and you."

"Me?"

The grey stone of Saint Magdalene church came into view.

"Explain yourself," I said, my voice still dry with a touch of the witch's cackle.

"Don't like to say nothin', miss."

Boots slowed the motorcar to a crawl, his face turned towards the churchyard. For a long while, he stared through the headstones towards the Bagington Hall family plot and the spot where Miss Antoinette lay.

I followed his gaze.

Under the dim afternoon light, it was bleak and cold and lonely.

I tried to make a little conversation to help loosen his lips. "Such a peaceful place to rest on a summer's day, don't you think?"

"Wouldn't know about that, miss."

"Don't you find churchyards relaxing?"

"Not especially, miss."

"I like to practise my penmanship while seated on a bench or leaning against a headstone."

His eyes fastened on mine. "Prefers it inside the church, on me knees in the pews asking for forgiveness."

The church bell chimed for the quarter to the hour. His body stiffened, and he let out a cry. "Gonna be late. I'll be for it for sure with Mr Withers, now."

I said, "Don't worry. I'll tell him it was my fault."

Boots relaxed.

I took my chance. "Do tell what people are saying about me? It's not right that it should be kept from my ears."

Boots sighed. "Suppose you'll hear it soon enough, miss."

"Go on," I said. "I'll not hold it against you."

He spoke fast, the words flying out like arrows from a bow. "Some at Bagington Hall says you brought a curse with you. Others, that you and your uncle are in league with the devil."

Startled, I cried, "What on earth are you talking about?"

Boots twisted his head, bloodshot eyes wide open. "Since you showed up on Monday with all this talk of a staffing agency, there has been nothing but bloody murder and mayhem at Bagington Hall. The talk is of witchcraft and a curse over your business. Ain't NO worker in Norfolk will put their name down for THAT."

Chapter 47

I WAS AMAZED TO SEE Dolly Trimmings at the entrance to the carriage house when I arrived. I was even more astonished at what she wore—a plain, black dress with a white apron, and on her head, a simple, frilled white cap.

Before the motorcar had pulled to a stop, her plump hand was tugging at the door handle.

"Miss Darling, is that you?"

Dolly's birdlike eyes twitched. The wide hippopotamus mouth stretched upward at the edges. She climbed into the vehicle and threw her arms about me. There was a strong whiff of plum wine about her person. Her hug was that of a bear.

"Oh Gawd, yes, yes, it is you!"

You would have thought we were long-lost sisters, separated at birth, and reunited after twenty years. You would have thought her friendly shout came from snatches of shared nostalgic childhood recollections. But I'd met Dolly Trimmings for the very first time on Monday. Today was Saturday. Our acquaintance was less than a week old.

I could sense that something was wrong. "What's going on?"

"Miss Darling, I shall walk you to the house where Her Ladyship awaits your presence." Dolly twisted a strand of loose hair.

"Boots, you go about your business. Miss Darling is in my capable hands."

"But I have orders to walk Miss Darling to—"

"Don't you dare argue," Dolly snapped.

Boots hesitated.

"Be off with you," she cried violently, stamping her foot. "Else it'll be the horsewhip again for you. And now Sir Sandoe is dead, I'll 'ave to do it myself!"

Boots' face flushed; his eyes became saucers. "Got to check the coal stores then work on the stables, and Mr Withers wants the motorcar washed, waxed, and cleaned from top to bottom before I begin my inside duties. Suppose it'll be all right."

Dolly grabbed my arm. "This way, Miss Darling. We must hurry, else you'll be late."

Once we got some distance from the carriage house and turned onto the gravel path that ran alongside the main house, I said, "Don't you think you were rather rough with Boots?"

Dolly's voice was low and controlled. "Oh Gawd, yes. It's the only language the lad understands. Nothing like a good horsewhipping to keep 'im in line."

I didn't agree. Violence against domestic staff led to simmering resentment that might boil over at any moment. I changed the subject. "Where are your pearls?"

Dolly's right hand flew to her throat as if grasping for a necklace, then she shrugged. It was supposed to be a careless gesture, but something in the slump of the shoulders and tremble on her wide lips told another story.

"Mere trinkets and baubles," she said flatly. Her lips thinned, and she spoke in the tone of Lady Herriman. "Pearls are best left in the depths of the sea rather than slung with garish vulgarity around the neck, don't you think?"

"I admire your philosophy," I said. But there was more to this. Dolly Trimmings wasn't the sort of woman to easily give up trinkets and baubles.

Then it struck me.

With Boots in a pressed suit, and Dolly dressed in a maid's uniform, there was only one logical explanation. Bagington Hall was in mourning for the passing of Sir Sandoe.

I said, "Your outfit is a touching tribute and a mark of deep respect."

"Practical too," she said tartly. "Pearls don't go with work clothes."

Having got over my initial shock of Dolly's plain outfit, I wanted inside information about Lady Herriman's demeanour. "How is Her Ladyship this evening?"

Dolly raised a hand to straighten her cap. "Been her loyal servant for years; ain't no one but me can put up with her. But I've 'ad enough. When me gold shares come in, I'll give me notice."

That wasn't what I expected, but the mention of gold pricked my interest. I said, "Any news from Peru?"

"Oh yes!" She placed a finger to her lips and lowered her voice. "I hear they've struck gold in two mines, and I've got my lot of shares, thanks to Sir Sandoe. The discovery will be in the *Norfolk News* next weekend, I suppose."

I kept my voice level, not wanting to give away my growing sense of excitement. "Are you quite sure... about the gold discovery?"

Dolly rubbed her chin. "That's what I heard from Withers, and he knows everything about Bagington Hall, all the secrets an' all."

As soon as the opportunity arose, I'd corner the sleazy butler and pepper him with questions about the gold mines and also Miss Antoinette. This time he'd not wriggle away without answering.

I allowed myself to relax a little. Uncle Tristan's investments were sound, Father's savings secure, and Nancy's future no longer in peril. Still, I'd request the bank cheque from Lady Herriman and have Uncle deposit it first thing Monday morning in Norwich.

Dolly's hand suddenly shot out and gripped so tight on to my arm I almost yelled out in pain. "Oh, Miss Darling, the shock of everything has knocked Her Ladyship right off her rocker."

I broke free of her grip but sensed an undercurrent of nervousness. "Two deaths in a week is a tough challenge."

"You don't understand!" Dolly stopped. A sheen of perspiration covered her fat upper lip. "There is to be no period of mourning for Sir Sandoe."

I frowned. "What do you mean?"

"Sir Sandoe is to be laid to rest this Wednesday by Vicar Humberstone in a common plot without a headstone."

"Dear God," I murmured. "I know Sir Sandoe and Lady Herriman didn't see eye to eye, but surely..."

"The stress has been too great for Her Ladyship," said Dolly, hurrying ahead. "And there are those who will take advantage of the situation. Please keep up; we don't have much time."

I hurried after Dolly and said, "But a common plot, what can it mean?"

Dolly said, "Her Ladyship's been as secretive as a fox planning an attack on the henhouse."

"Lady Herriman is bound to be a little fragile in mood," I said. "Let us not forget it has only been a day since... well, and the police are looking for Frank Perry. All that is required is a little patience, charity, and goodwill towards the woman. At times like these, I find it best just to listen."

Dolly stopped, took a deep breath, and shrugged. "I'd listen, but Her Ladyship refuses to speak with me. Been cast out like a used dishcloth, I 'ave." Again, she gripped my arm, her forehead beaded with sweat, face white and expressionless. "There is something else you should know."

"Yes," I said, easing my arm from her firm grip. "What is it?"

Dolly's voice dropped so low I had to strain to hear the words. "Withers is stealing from Bagington Hall. Please have Her Ladyship ring for me, and I'll give her the details. I'm sure she will listen to you." She let out a piggish snort and began to run. "Come on, else you'll be late."

Chapter 48

AS WE HURRIED ALONG a dim hallway, questions tumbled around my mind. How long had Dolly known about Withers' thievery? Why had she waited until now to reveal it? And why to me? And then there was the business about Sir Sandoe's funeral. It just didn't make any sense.

Dolly Trimmings moved remarkably fast for a large woman, her heavy breaths like a donkey pulling a cart. I struggled to keep up. We were at the door of Lady Herriman's antechamber before the first question came from my lips.

Dolly applied a timid knock.

"Come in," called Lady Herriman in a high-pitched, fruity voice reminiscent of a London stage actress calling to her lover. "I've been awaiting your arrival."

"Go ahead," said Dolly, giving me a gentle shove in the back. "She'll be delighted when she realises it is you. I'll wait outside, and you can call me in when you tell her about Withers."

It took a moment for my eyes to adjust to the gloom. Gradually, the edges of furniture came into view. Next, the large glass cases—the lion, tiger, and leopard in full stride. Then, at last, I saw Lady Herriman.

She sat in the darkest corner, on a high-backed seat with golden swirls, velvet, and leather. It was more throne than chair. And she was queenlike and graceful in a mauve, silk gown with a little diamond-encrusted tiara perched atop her exuberant Elizabethan wig. In one hand she held an oversized goblet. With the other, she gave a regal wave. At her side, a little table on which rested a giant leather-bound Bible and her lorgnette spectacles.

"Miss Darling? I expected another. Not to worry, you are here in good time. Please, take a seat." She waved at a claw-footed velvet settee. A flimsy, black dress with a little white apron and frilly cap lay loosely over one arm. "There is much to discuss."

I watched Her Ladyship closely as I settled into my seat. Her ancient eyes were bright and clear, her powdered cheeks tinged with rose, and her thin lips curved up at the edges. I hadn't expected sackcloth and ashes, but there was not a shred of anything resembling distress in her face. She appeared quite the opposite. If the woman was in mourning for Sir Sandoe, she hid it well.

As if to confirm my thoughts, Lady Herriman said, "Despite the ghastly events of the last twenty-four hours, I've had the best night's sleep in years." She took a long, slow gulp from the goblet all the while her eyes fixed on my face. "One must make the best of things."

The woman appeared happy, almost joyous. What happened to the sour toad? I wanted to ask but remembered Uncle Tristan's admonition to eat humble pie in her presence. I said, "That is so admirable. When life throws a terrible blow, weaker beings go to pieces."

"Oh, I do so enjoy our little audiences," she crowed, placing a thin, spindly hand on the Bible. "The Lord delivers justice in his own time. There is no escape from the might of his hand."

"Still," I said, choosing my words with care, "Sir Sandoe's demise must have come as a terrible shock."

The thin lips tugged upward, creasing the powdered cheeks. "Nothing less than the wretched man deserved." In an exaggerated movement, she reached for her lorgnette spectacles, placed them to her eyes, and gazed down at the floor. "And I suspect it is rather hot where he is. The funeral is on Wednesday. You'll attend?"

I'd had my fill of funerals but said, "Of course, I will be there to pay my respects."

Lady Herriman placed the lorgnette spectacles on the side table and took a sip from the goblet. Her thin lips smacked together as if the taste was especially gratifying. "I will lay Sir Sandoe to rest in a paupers' plot, an unmarked grave."

I could hardly believe my ears. Dolly was right! I sat very still, eager to know more, my lips pressed tight shut.

"The man was not from the Bagington lineage," said Lady Herriman. "An interloper from Surrey! His sinful corpse shall not rest for eternity in the Bagington Hall family plot. I made that clear to the vicar."

"I see," I murmured, wondering if perhaps there was not another reason. One related to the death of Miss Antoinette and the disappearance of Lady Sandoe. I took a deep breath and said, "Did Sir Sandoe offer any explanation for the disappearance of Lady Sandoe?"

I stared at her, apprehension rippling through me like a wave on the beach.

Lady Herriman got up and threw down the Bible onto the side table. Her lorgnette spectacles danced in a little circle.

"I hope, dear child, you are not trying to play the role of a detective. That belongs to men and those employed in the local constabulary. Snooping around is one of the many faults of Dolly Trimmings. That and her drinking, and her tittle-tattle. Are you a snoop, Miss Darling?"

"Oh no, Lady Herriman," I said humbly. "Only curious about the workings of the household. Such information helps Tristan's Hands find suitable workers."

"Then you'll need to understand that Sir Sandoe was not well liked by the staff. Nor did I ever take to the horrid little man. Neither did Miss Antoinette." Lady Herriman's voice became shrill. "The only person who saw a flicker of something in his wretched soul was Lady Sandoe and then only until she found out he was a sponge. If I'd had the strength of a man, I'd have taken the horsewhip to him!"

Stunned at her outburst, I changed the subject. "A property of this size requires a large staff. Will you need additional workers?"

Lady Herriman lowered herself onto the throne, glanced towards the door as if she were expecting someone, and said, "Let us discuss that later. There is a rather important matter that has come to my attention." She paused and fixed me with a sharp eye. "A bank cheque found on Sir Sandoe's writing bureau."

I shifted in my seat.

Lady Herriman continued, "Drawn on his personal bank account in Norwich and made out to Mr Harbottle." She reached down for the Bible, flipped it open, and retrieved a long ornate slip of paper.

Sit still, I told myself. Remain perfectly still and don't say a word. She'll give it to you if you just don't speak. I held my breath and prayed.

"Please give this to your uncle," said Lady Herriman, waving the bank cheque like a Chinese fan.

I darted forward, grasped it from her hand, then embarrassed, uttered, "Thank you."

"Oh, the eagerness of youth!" Lady Herriman let out an amused chuckle. "Mr Harbottle shall frame it—"

"As you wish," I interrupted, ready for dinner to be over.

"And place it on his office wall as a permanent remembrance. And I hope every day when he comes into the office, he pauses and reflects on his foolishness."

"Eh?"

"Certain rumours have been swirling around Bagington Hall," said Lady Herriman. "Unfounded rumours, which, I regret to say, have their source in Sir Sandoe."

I said nothing as a sense of foreboding tiptoed along my spine.

Lady Herriman straightened her shoulders, and with a superior tilt of the head said, "Miss Darling, I hope that worthless bank cheque will remind your uncle to henceforth avoid idle speculation."

"Worthless?"

"Sir Sandoe poured his gold investors' money into the gaming table, the horse track, and the greyhound races. Neither of his betting ventures, I might add, met with any measure of success. His bankers visited this morning. I made it crystal clear that the Bagington Hall estate will not stand behind any of his enormous gambling losses."

Chapter 49

"MISS DARLING, I AM to remarry," announced Lady Herriman in a birdlike chirp.

My concentration was focused on the bank cheque, the nonexistent gold mines, and Sir Sandoe's gambling debts. I gazed at the ornate slip of worthless paper in a dazed wonder and was only vaguely aware of Lady Herriman standing to her feet.

"You may congratulate me now," she said.

Still, my mind was elsewhere. The loss of Uncle Tristan's life savings would kill him. Or, at least, he would make so much noise, others might think he was under savage attack. And then there was Father's losses—at his age, everything gone! I could scarcely think about that. With no money, there was no choice for me but to remain in Cromer until I was able to raise enough to return to London.

Oh bother!

On the edge of blind panic, my mind raced. There were no jobs in this tiny village, and the agricultural strike made matters worse—no one was hiring until things settled down. How would I pay the rent? I wondered if there was room for two in Uncle's shed in the vegetable patch and if Mrs Banbury would complain.

But as bad as it was, things were not totally hopeless. There was still one trick up my sleeve. I said, "Advanced payment for Tristan's Hand's services, why don't you write the cheque now?"

"Dear child, have you been listening?"

"Sorry, Lady Herriman. It is just we need to discuss business."

"That is what I've been attempting to do." She sighed, straightened the tiara, and said, "The young are so easily distracted; the mind flits from thing to thing like a butterfly. Now are you going to congratulate me?"

"Indeed," I said, still thinking how to break the news to Uncle Tristan. "For what?"

"The wedding."

"Wedding.... married... to whom?" This was too much; I couldn't think clearly.

Lady Herriman placed her lorgnette spectacles to her face and studied me for a few moments. Then she took a sip from the goblet. "It is to be Thursday, in Norwich, the day after we lay Sir Sandoe to rest. Twenty-four hours between grave and altar seems a suitable period, whatever Vicar Humberstone's protestations." She left the sentence hanging, raised a finger, and pointed at the arm of the settee. "Now, child, why don't you slip into that chambermaid's outfit. You can't serve dinner dressed like that."

I gasped as if the contents of her goblet had been thrown over me. "Pardon?"

"Take the dress, apron, and cap, and return when you are suitably attired." Lady Herriman spoke in a sharp tone as one might to an errant dog. "There is a small closet along the hall."

I stared, eyes wide, blinking.

"There will be a period of training, but you are an intelligent child. Oh, we shall enjoy our little audiences together just before supper every evening. And you shall sing from my little Victorian hymnal, just like Miss Antoinette used to."

Chapter 50

"AFTER THE MEAL," LADY Herriman said, "I shall be in a better position to assess your ability and discuss my expectations."

I sat very still, mouth agape, shocked and bewildered, eyes bugging at Lady Herriman on her throne with that tremendous white wig and diamond tiara.

As I remained motionless, I thought I heard a commotion in the passage outside.

"Now hurry along and get changed," snapped Lady Herriman. "And you shall regale us with a song after dessert."

Suddenly it all became clear. Lady Herriman wanted me to serve as her chambermaid, and as part of the deal, I must sing for my supper!

With a growing sense of distress, I thought about Uncle Tristan. He had urged me to bring home the bacon. I gulped. Not only was there no bacon, but if Lady Herriman heard my singing voice, I wouldn't even get any supper. My stomach growled.

Oh bother!

With steely determination, I pushed everything from my mind: the gold, the bank cheque, the death of Miss Antoinette, the bloody slaying of Sir Sandoe, and Lady Herriman's insane babbling about a wedding.

Mind cleared, I began to think quickly. But the first vivid realisation was almost crushing. Uncle Tristan was penniless. Father's savings gone, and I was without employment and in need of money to escape Cromer.

An angry shout from the passageway followed loud thwacks. As the dull thud repeatedly sounded, the answer to my immediate problem formed shape—Tristan's Hands!

I stepped forward. "Lady Herriman, I am not here to work as a servant but to supply your household with staff. Now, if you require a personal chambermaid, Tristan's Hands can help."

"Dear child," began Lady Herriman in a sour tone, "I hardly see the difference. After all, it is I who pay, and so it is I who choose. And I choose you as a chambermaid. Now get changed, it is almost time for dinner."

There was an authoritative knock on the door.

I let out a breath, thankful for the interruption. It would give me time to think. There was a solution, and I knew I would find it.

I closed my eyes for an instant. You can do this, Maggie, I told myself. You can sell Lady Herriman on Tristan's Hands and will leave Bagington Hall with a big fat bank cheque.

My eyes opened.

I was determined.

I was ready.

"Come," called Lady Herriman, rising to her feet. Her voice was high pitched and feminine.

I looked on with undisguised astonishment as Withers strode into the room. He wore a high-end, pinstriped, three-piece suit. Under his arm, he carried a horsewhip.

The former butler hesitated for a moment as if his eyes required time to adjust to the dim light. Then as Lady Herriman stood, left arm outstretched, he scurried across the room, took her withered hand, and planted a kiss on the back of it.

"Louisa, a spot of bother in the passageway," Withers said, straightening up. "Dolly Trimmings was snooping about. The thieving toad had her ear against the door. Full of plum wine again! Well, I gave her a good talking to followed by the horsewhip. Nothing to worry your pretty mind over."

"Oh, darling, that is so masterful," crooned Lady Herriman, her eyes dancing with delight. "I should have taken the whip to her years ago. Look, her replacement is here to serve us dinner."

Withers turned, and for the first time learned of my presence. He ran a finger over his thin hairline moustache. "Oh, how delightful. Maggie, isn't it?"

The sleazy man bloody well knew who I was. "Miss Darling, to you," I said with an air of hostility.

"Ah, yes, Miss Darling." Withers rolled my name around his mouth as if tasting a fine wine. "From Mr Harbottle's staffing agency?"

Infuriated at the man's arrogance, I got straight to the point. "I'm here to discuss the staffing needs of Bagington Hall. Lady Herriman needs a chambermaid, and I—"

Withers raised a hand. "Tell Mr Harbottle we have no use for Tristan's Hands and will no longer require his services."

It took a moment for his words to sink in. I gasped for air, eyes bulging, throat too dry to speak.

"That is the other item of business we were to discuss," added Lady Herriman. "But there is no more to be said on the matter, so let us move on."

It was all over for Uncle Tristan's staffing business. Ahead lay a miserable life for Uncle eking out a living as a poet in a shed at the bottom of a garden next to the vegetable patch. And I'd have to return to London with empty pockets.

I could not let that happen.

I stood and said, "Now listen here—"

But Withers ignored my words and turned to face Lady Herriman. "Take a seat, my love," he said in a soft voice. "A lady of your fine breeding must be comfortable at all times."

Lady Herriman began to sit, caught sight of her own reflection in a tall mirror above one of the gilt-legged console tables against the wall, and remained on her feet. "Do you think this gown ages me?"

"Oh, no," replied Withers. "Mauve is rather fetching in this light, reminds one of plums under a harvest moon."

Lady Herriman turned to face the mirror and surveyed herself. She lowered her eyelids and drew her thin lips into a pout. With the tips of her heavily jewelled fingers, she delicately touched her powdered, hollowed cheeks. "I thought about adding pearls, but they are best left in the depths of the sea rather than slung with garish vulgarity around the neck, don't you think?"

"Indeed, indeed," replied Withers.

"But, perhaps," began Lady Herriman, " I shall pack one or two pearl necklaces for our tour of Europe. They seem much less vulgar on the continent." She leaned forward, her spine straightening. "And I shall wear pearls on our wedding night!"

"Ah yes... the wedding... night," echoed Withers.

If I hadn't been paying attention, I would have missed it. An almost imperceptible shudder. It began with a slight tremble of his shoulders and slithered like a snake along his spine. When the tremor reached his legs, they shook, and his feet shuffled back and forth like a clog dancer.

"Dr Swensen suggests travel," Withers said. "No farther than Norwich... until your heart strengthens. No excitement, none whatsoever. It's the doctor's orders. Have you an ample supply of sleeping pills?"

"Hang Dr Swensen!" Lady Herriman eased herself onto the throne. "Together, we shall enjoy Paris and visit Monsieur Bonhomme's exquisite jewellery studio off the Champs-Élysées. Then Rome and Madrid. A grand tour of Europe. Our days shall be filled with finery and our nights with passion. And Miss Darling shall come with us."

"As you wish." Withers, hand shaking, slipped a pendant from his pocket. It swayed back and forth. "But let us... follow the pendant... make our plans... feeling sleepy now... after the wedding... fast asleep."

Lady Herriman's eyelids drooped. "As you wish," she said, her head lolling to one side. "As you..."

"Louisa?" Withers whispered. "Are you awake?"

Nothing.

Withers spun around.

"Sit!" he commanded.

Shocked, I sat, my left hand rested on the chambermaid's dress, white apron, and cap. My heart raced as anger pulsed through my veins.

When I was calm enough to think clearly, I said, "What on earth do you mean by hypnotising Her Ladyship into marriage?"

Several seconds of silence passed before Withers spoke. "From now on," he began in a deep voice, "I shall refer to you as Maggie, and I am to be referred to as His Lordship. Is that clear?"

"Answer my question," I said, voice shrill.

He crossed the carpet to the heavily draped window and pulled back the curtain to peer out through a chink.

Light flooded the room.

He spoke without turning. "Soon, I shall be Lord of Bagington Hall. Lady Herriman requires another chambermaid, and you are to be it. As for Dolly Trimmings, she has served her purpose and will leave at first light on Monday. Might even give her another horsewhipping to send her on her way."

"You blaggard!" I snapped.

Withers let the curtain drop. Gloom descended over the room. He turned around, legs planted wide, arms behind his back.

"Until then, she is to live outside the main house in the stable loft." He paused, ran a finger over his hairline moustache, and smiled. "Maggie, you are to tell Dolly the news. Then you shall return to serve dinner."

Suddenly my mouth became dry. "Now just you wait—"

"Eighty-five shillings a week as Lady Herriman's chambermaid." Withers reached into his top pocket, pulled out a watch, and looked up. "You have sixty seconds to accept."

Eighty-five shillings a week! That would be enough to pay the rent, send money to Father, and save too. It would allow Uncle Tristan time to rebuild his business.

"I'm sure," said Withers, reaching into another pocket and pulling out the pendant, "you will be a loyal replacement for Dolly and an accepting student of my teachings."

My eyes moved back and forth, watching the little metallic disc as it swung from left to right.

"A very faithful replacement..." he continued in a restful voice, "and compliant of all my instructions..."

Withers' words sunk in and rolled around my mind as I thought of all that had happened. In a matter of hours, everything had crumbled—Uncle Tristan's investments, Father's savings, Nancy's future. The chambermaid job offered an easy solution. With eighty-five shillings a week, I could begin to remake my life.

"Accept the offer, and all will be well. Take the work and live a peaceful life..." Withers continued to speak in a low, soothing voice. The pendant swung back and forth. "Soon you will have the money to build a better future."

I let my eyelids droop.

"Yes." I could use the job to clamber back onto my feet, save a little money, and over time, things would improve.

It was then I remembered what Mr Pritchard had said the day I started behind the counter in his pie-and-mash shop." I shall pay you above the going rate, and soon you will have the money to build a better future."

Then came the subtle hints about feeling lonely despite his long-suffering wife and seven children. Next came the accidental touches, and when that did not ignite my interest, the outright piggish demands that I become his sweetheart.

I opened my eyes and stood.

With a casual voice, devoid of the emotions churning around in my stomach, I said, "It is kind you think so highly of me and that you wish me to serve in this household at such an elevated position." I took a deep breath. "But I cannot accept your offer. I am clerk to Mr Harbottle and intend to remain so. Tristan's Hands does not permit our staff to be hypnotised, beaten, or otherwise abused by their employers. We shall seek alternative clients."

"Such a pity," Withers said with a sigh, placing the pendant back into his pocket. "I was rather looking forward to availing myself of your personal services."

As I turned to leave, I noticed Lady Herriman was leaning forward on her throne, eyes wide open and alert.

Chapter 51

IT WAS AFTER 9 P.M. when I stood by the bedroom window in Mrs Rusbridger's boarding house. A single oil lamp cast a gentle glow into the darkened chamber. Outside, a full moon shone in the long garden, a gorgeous buttery lantern in a greyish magenta sky.

The conversations with Lady Herriman, Dolly Trimmings, and Withers tumbled around my mind. Why had Her Ladyship agreed to cast out Dolly so readily? What about the wedding? And what did Withers know about the murder of Miss Antoinette and the disappearance of Lady Sandoe? My brain worked hard trying to piece it all together but found no answers.

After a while, I thought about Father and Uncle Tristan, but no matter how hard I searched, there was no sign of a silver lining to the money situation. Everything was lost, but it was too late to visit Uncle Tristan. It was well after dark. I gazed up at the sky.

"At least he'll have a peaceful sleep."

First thing tomorrow morning I'd walk to Mrs Banbury's garden, find his shed, and share the bad tidings. Tonight, though, I'd watch the moon and think.

A hunger pang growled across my stomach, intensified, and multiplied. I clenched my jaw. I hadn't eaten all day. And at this hour, the boarding house kitchen was closed.

"Not even a cup of tea," I muttered bitterly.

That the gold mines in Peru were a sham wasn't a great surprise. But a deep sense of injustice niggled. For Uncle Tristan, for my father, and for all the other investors who'd suffered losses in Sir Sandoe's phantom scheme.

Again, my stomach rumbled.

"Oh bother!"

When I focused on something else, the pangs eased. I closed my eyes. Frank Perry's image filled my mind. The dagger, Sir Sandoe crumpled on the ground, and the letter. I saw it all in vivid detail.

My eyes snapped open.

To my surprise, I felt a deep sense of injustice for Sir Sandoe. Whatever his crimes, he didn't deserve to die at the end of a jagged blade. Cold-blooded murder was no righter than stealing.

A gentle tap-tap on the bedroom door scattered my thoughts.

The door creaked open.

Mrs Rusbridger came hurrying into the room. She carried a tray on which rested a large plate next to a silver tankard.

"Brought you a bit of supper, seeing as you missed breakfast and dinner." Swiftee trotted at her side. "Thought I'd bring the little fellow as he ain't seen you all day."

"Thank you," I gushed, grateful for the food. "What delights have you rustled up from your wonderful kitchen?"

She wiped her hands on the apron. "Cold swan with duck lard on a bed of roast nettles." The corners of her mouth twitched with tiny upward movements. "And turnip juice to wash it down."

"Oh!"

Mrs Rusbridger's lips broke out into a wide grin. "Was only joking, me dear. But I heard from Cook that's what was on the menu at Bagington Hall. Ain't nobody eats roast swan about these parts except Lady Herriman, and turnip juice gives me the runs. Did you get to taste the sparrow pudding?"

"No, no," I said, nose wrinkling in disgust. "The fact is I didn't sample a morsel of Lady Herriman's Victorian delights."

"God bless ya." Mrs Rusbridger placed the tray on the writing desk. "Well, sit down. Eat up. Cold ham with buttered bread, cheese, and pickles, washed down with a tankard of cider. That'll help keep ya till morning."

My stomach rumbled in appreciation. The boarding house felt more like home every day.

"Sit and eat," said Mrs Rusbridger, pointing at the chair.

I sat.

Mrs Rusbridger walked over to the window, and as I ate, peered out into the garden. "Harvest moon tonight, like daylight out there. Bet Swiftee catches a mouse or two."

"Mmm, guess so."

As I drained the last drop from the tankard, Mrs Rusbridger turned and with a sad smile said, "Is it true?"

I put the tankard down. There was no point denying it. If Mrs Rusbridger knew of Uncle's financial reversal, so would all of Cromer.

"Yes, it's true. Uncle Tristan—"

"My God, it ain't right!" Mrs Rusbridger clapped her hands in annoyance. "A funeral on Wednesday and wedding Thursday, and Miss Antoinette only just laid to rest with Sir Sandoe's killer still on the run. Cook told me everything, but I couldn't believe me ears."

"Oh," I said, realising she was talking about Lady Herriman's wedding. "It is rather soon."

"Soon! If Her Ladyship were younger, I'd think she were up the spout. But she's older than my grandma. Only thing I can think is that Withers 'as put something in her food to make her mind turn funny, but Cook swears that ain't the case."

I thought about the silver pendant and Withers' soothing hypnotic words but didn't want to add fuel to the Cromer gossip fire, so I kept quiet on that detail and said, "It's a real mystery. What do you think lies at the bottom of all this?"

"Sir Sandoe's murder."

"Pardon?"

Mrs Rusbridger said, "If I didn't know better, I'd think Withers put Frank Perry up to it."

I opened my eyes wide. "But how did Withers pull off such a trick, and why would Frank Perry agree?"

"Revenge!" Mrs Rusbridger paused, her voice dropping to a whisper. "Everyone knows Mr Perry was sweet on Miss Antoinette. And as for Withers, I know his type. Wants to be lord over Bagington Hall."

I'd seen that much for myself and had to agree.

Mrs Rusbridger continued, "Me thinks Withers let Frank Perry into Bagington Hall and told him where he could find Sir Sandoe. The evil toad might 'ave even given Frank the dagger."

"But how did Frank evade the staff and get into the scullery yard?"

"Easy. 'Tis a large old house, lots of hidden passageways and stairwells. Withers knows them better than the master." Her face creased in concern. "It won't be long after the wedding bells that Lady Herriman ends up in Saint Magdalene's cemetery: mark my words. Then Withers will 'ave it all and rule Bagington Hall with an iron fist."

I considered that for a moment. The man was devious with a violent temper. What wouldn't he do to get what he wanted? With power over the estate, his wickedness would be limitless.

I said, "What do you know about Withers' background?"

Mrs Rusbridger's eyes narrowed as she recalled the details. "Years ago, he worked in a travelling circus—as a clown." She said the word as if it had a foul taste. "Ever wondered about all that powder on Her Ladyship's face?"

I had but kept my mouth shut and waited.

"Miserable sods, clowns—devious too." As if to emphasise the point, she jabbed her index finger in the air. "Withers had a side enterprise as a hypnotist then worked as a fortune teller but couldn't make a go of it."

I let that sink in and settle. There was not much doubt about Withers' desire to advance himself. And that was almost impossible in the ridged British class system. The surprising thing was by next Thursday he'd have pulled it off. I didn't like the man or his method but couldn't help but admire his determination to better himself.

"Nowadays," said Mrs Rusbridger as the corners of her mouth twitched upward, "I hear he gives Lady Herriman makeup tips while swinging his deceitful pendant. He's a slimy toad, he is. Now I thinks about it, wouldn't be surprised if he hypnotised the old hen into marriage." She shuddered. "Like I say, clowns are devious little buggers."

I said nothing because it would have been pointless. Withers was a blighter and wicked with it.

Swiftee clambered into my lap. I stroked the kitten's chin. He purred.

Mrs Rusbridger chuckled. "Seems like you've conquered the cat allergies."

The woman was a master at changing the subject. I didn't mind and said, "Apple cider vinegar. Three times a day. Got it from Mrs Mullins, and it works."

She nodded, pondered for a moment, then her voice dropped an octave. "Since you're to be Lady Herriman's new chambermaid, I hope you won't forget old Mrs Rusbridger and drop by once in a while to update me on the goings-on at Bagington Hall."

She wanted to add me to her network of chattering women. They were the grapevine along which gossip flowed. It was an honour to be asked, but I had to let her know the situation.

I said, "Alas, I did not accept the job offer."

"Don't blame you. Her Ladyship works the staff like slaves. I hear she orders the horsewhip to the laggards. It ain't right. And if there were more jobs in these parts, no one would put up with it. Miss Darling, you're too intelligent a woman to take a position like that."

When Mrs Rusbridger left the room, I returned to the bedroom window. The glittering moonlight illuminated the garden like a lantern. As I watched the shadows dancing, something niggled at the back of my mind. The moon dipped behind a cloud plunging the room into darkness penetrated only by the sputtering glow of the oil lamp. The niggle became a loud thump that hit me hard and quick.

When the moon reappeared, I pulled on my coat, cloche hat, and set out towards Mrs Banbury's garden and the shed by the vegetable patch. I had to tell Uncle Tristan of his misfortune before word got to him on the Cromer gossip grapevine.

Chapter 52

I STOOD AT THE ENTRANCE of Mrs Rusbridger's boarding house, staring at the long, narrow gravel path that led to the lane. The salty scent from the sea mingled with the tang of oak trees, hedgerows, and grass.

The moon disappeared behind a wall of black clouds. As I waited for it to reappear, I wondered at the wisdom of creeping about Cromer at night. In London, the dark hours attracted criminals like a moth to a light. It wasn't wise to walk the streets of the capital city alone after sunset.

"Not London," I muttered, as the buttery globe appeared from behind the clouds. "This is Cromer, a sleepy Norfolk village." The most I expected to meet on my journey was a rabbit, owl, or maybe a fox.

With soft steps, I turned onto the gravel path that led to the gate at the end of the garden. I paused for a moment to take in the lane, lined with hedgerows and oak trees, and the fields beyond. It was less than three miles to Mrs Banbury's cottage, past the church, Hilda Ogbern's house, then right onto a dirt lane. I could do that inside of an hour. Once there, I'd share the news and be back at the boarding house before 1 a.m.

The gate swung shut behind me with a loud creak. I glanced warily over my shoulder, half expecting to see Mrs Rusbridger on the doorstep, arms folded, scowling. But the rough grey stone of the house was in darkness, the only movement, the gentle swaying shadows of clematis and tea roses illuminated by the glow of a solitary oil lamp.

The light waxed and waned as more clouds marched across the face of the moon. The wind picked up. Leaves skittered in mad circles. The hoot of an owl echoed above the sound of wind rustling through the trees. I quickened my pace, pulling the coat tight about me and kept to the edge of the lane, close to the hedgerows.

After perhaps forty-five minutes, the tower of Saint Magdalene came into view. It was then I considered the best approach to share the news with Uncle Tristan. I didn't want to say anything rash that would throw him into a blind panic. But my appearance in the dead of night would herald bad news before my lips spoke the words.

The minutes flashed by as I turned the matter over and over in my head. There was no solution. The best I could do was remain calm. Together we would work out a plan.

At the iron gates at the entrance of the churchyard, I stopped. The dark trees gloomed down, their shadows dancing like sprites. Something flickered between the headstones. I stared wide eyed as a long shadow crept close to the ground.

Instinct took over. I crouched low against the railings. The scent of dusty soil mingled with the sharp tang of grass. This is silly. There would be no one in the graveyard. Why were my legs shaking?

The moon dipped behind a cloud casting the church into darkness. For several moments, I scanned the space. At the far side of the graveyard, a tall, dark jumble stood above the headstones. It might have been a prayer chapel. It was from that direction a scraping, crackling sound echoed in the darkness.

I couldn't tell what made the noise. The longer I squatted in the shadows, the less sure I became. It might only have been the wind rustling leaves.

I kept still, forced myself to stare. Ahead and to the left of the tall, dark jumble, a shape came into view. It scurried on all fours.

"Fox," I mumbled. "Must have trapped a rabbit."

I waited.

The moon broke free of the clouds. What I had taken as a prayer chapel turned out to be a stone monument with a tall cross yellowed with moss. To one side, the creature snorted.

Wait! It was too large to be a fox. Much too large for that. It moved like a wolf.

Suddenly the air seemed perfectly still. For a terrible moment, I thought of Black Shuck and curses and death. The pounding of my heart was so hard it was a continuous rumble in my ears.

The creature lifted its head, tilting it in my direction. The moonlight reflected a yellow glint in its eyes. It remained very still, staring. With almost imperceptible movements, it eased forward, then with long galloping strides, raced in my direction.

"Dobbin, sit!" I commanded. "Hilda Ogbern won't be happy that you've escaped again."

But the dog didn't sit; he rolled over.

Breathless, I rubbed his stomach while I collected my thoughts.

After several minutes of play, I rose to my feet. Dobbin trotted at my side until we came to the Ogbern's cottage. The narrow wooden gate swung back and forth in the breeze.

"So that's how you got out, eh?"

I shooed the dog inside, eased the gate shut, and watched as he bounded off towards the front porch.

At last, I came to the lane that led to Mrs Banbury's. Soon the cottage came into view. There were laurel bushes and long grass on the other side of the path that led up to the main house. Through the garden gate, around the side of the house into the vegetable plot, and there at the end, stood Uncle Tristan's shed.

It was a ramshackle structure built from long strips of assorted wood. There were no windows, and the door hung at an angle as if fitted as an afterthought.

A bank of clouds rolled across the moon. Darkness engulfed the garden.

Suddenly I felt a cold breath on the back of my neck. A heavy hand clasped tight onto my shoulder.

"What are ya doin' 'ere?"

I spun around.

Frank Perry's flat eyes stared back. In his right hand, raised above his head, he held a long-handled, Victorian hunting dagger.

Chapter 53

THERE WAS A TENSE MOMENT of silence when I heard only the low thud of my heartbeat and the harsh whistle of the wind through the trees. I shrunk back, kept my eyes on the dagger, and prepared to scream or run or both.

Frank Perry repeated his question. "I said, what are ya doin' here?" His voice crackled with static, but he didn't move any closer.

Keep him talking, I told myself. That's what I did with the crazies in the pie-and-mash shop. Words seemed to sooth them, take their minds off their madness for a while. But what to say to a deranged killer?

"Frank, the police are looking for you." I had intended to say something else, something more pleasant.

"They'll never find me 'ere."

I snatched a furtive glance at the laurel bushes and long grass on the other side of the path that led up to the main house. I'd have to get closer to the building for my cries of help to carry above the wind. To do that, I needed a distraction.

"Run!" The word came from my mouth as a half shout, half command.

Frank didn't move.

"Run for your life, and you might escape the hangman's noose."

He glanced towards the house but still didn't move.

"Stay, and you'll be captured."

"I'll not leave Cromer until I'm done." He spat the words out with a sharpness that splintered the night air.

The moon drifted behind a bank of clouds. Everything became dark. A loud screech sounded. The door of the shed eased open.

"Maggie!"

Uncle Tristan appeared, his silhouette outlined against the faint glow of an oil lamp. "Quick, come inside, else we'll have the neighbours nosing around and then we'll be for it."

My eyes darted to Frank and back to Uncle Tristan. "But—"

"Ssshh!" Uncle Tristan whispered. "Hurry."

"After you, Miss Darling," said Frank, placing the dagger in his jacket pocket.

Chapter 54

THE HUT WAS DARK AND smelled of damp earth mingled with burnt tobacco. I took a shallow breath and gazed around. There was a little round table, two rough sacks that served as beds, a couple of stools and a chair.

My heart sunk. It was clear—Uncle Tristan was harbouring a man wanted for murder. Had the two men worked together to perform the grisly deed? I stifled a gasp, trying to think of an explanation.

I failed.

"Close the door, Frank." Uncle Tristan stooped to fiddle with the oil lamp. Its orange flame spluttered then intensified, bathing the small space with bright flecks of reds and yellows and whites like a morning sunrise.

"Righto." Frank closed the door then shuffled to the far side and eased onto a stool. He leaned back, resting his shoulders against the shack wall. His eyelids fluttered shut, revealing dark, sunken sockets.

Uncle Tristan sat on a low stool and directed me to the wooden chair. "Maggie, tell me everything about your meeting with Lady Herriman."

I said, "Why don't you explain what's going on here?"

"On second thought, just skip to the part about the bank cheque."

Frank let out a piggish snort. His head drooped.

I continued in a whisper, "Have you gone crazy? The man is wanted for murder."

"Did you ask about the bank cheque?"

"Uncle, have you lost your mind? You'll end up behind bars or worse." I kept my eyes on Frank Perry as I spoke.

"Don't mind Frank," said Uncle Tristan. "Nothing you say will ever cross his lips. Isn't that so, Frank?"

Frank's eyelids lifted. "Aye, ya secret is safe to the grave."

"Now, Maggie, please tell me what Lady Herriman had to say."

I kept my mouth shut for a moment and began to think. Uncle Tristan wasn't a murderer, crook, or otherwise bent to the devious. If Frank Perry was living in his shed, there had to be a good reason.

The wind picked up, slamming hard against the rickety walls.

I took an enormous breath, and with a raspy dryness in my throat, said, "The news isn't good."

Uncle pranced across the small space and took me by the shoulders. "I know it is bad tidings. Lady Herriman is as sharp as an axe. Did she offer to return only half? Do you have the bank cheque?"

"Yes, I do, but..."

"Rejoice! Rejoice! Rejoice! Half is better than I expected from the old witch. We'll fight over the remainder later." Uncle threw his arms in the air. "Last week down our alley came a toff. Nice old geezer with a nasty cough... Come on, Maggie, we're celebrating. Sing along with me..."

"The cheque is worthless."

He stopped mid prance, his arms above his head like antlers on a giant deer. "What are you saying?"

"Sir Sandoe's bankers visited Lady Herriman today. He died without a penny. The only thing he left was an insurmountable mountain of debt."

"But what of the gold mines?" Uncle Tristan's arms dropped to his side.

"There are no mines. Not in Peru or anywhere else. Sir Sandoe invested his backers' money in the gaming tables and lost. Uncle, everything's gone."

Uncle Tristan staggered back and collapsed onto the stool; his arms flew to the side hitting the wall. "This... this is despicable!"

"Yes it is," I agreed softly. I could not look at him. I bent my head and hid my face in my hands. I wanted to weep for Uncle Tristan, for Father, and for Nancy, but tears would not come. So I sat there helpless, listening to the muted silence of the spluttering oil lamp.

Uncle Tristan breathed in deeply and then out again. "Just one minute, Maggie, so I can think; clear my head; come up with a plan."

But after forty-seven minutes, he was still breathing heavily, and there were no signs of a plan, only the gentle crackle of the lamp.

"Uncle," I said at last, "I am afraid that is not the end."

His eyebrows shot up. "What more could there be?"

I closed my eyes as if I could shut out the truth with the darkness. "Lady Herriman has cancelled the contract with Tristan's Hands. Our agency has neither clients nor staff."

Uncle Tristan jerked to his feet, stood straight like a soldier on parade, and stared at me. Then as my words sunk in, his shoulders stooped.

"It's... as if we are... cursed! All we need now is for the wind to pick up and tear down this shed. Then I'll have nothing but the clothes on my back, and they belong to a dead man. Sir Sandoe's left me ruined!"

Another gust battered against the shed. Frank let out a piggish snort. His eyelids lifted.

"Wish I'd plunged the dagger into the evil sod's heart myself. I might have too, if the bugger weren't already dead when I found him."

Chapter 55

FRANK PERRY EASED ONTO his feet and walked to the entrance of the shed. There he stood for several minutes, hands behind his back, head tilted to one side, eyes half closed.

"Like I said, I wish I'd killed the bloody leach."

"Tell Maggie what happened," urged Uncle Tristan, his voice small and tired. "She might make sense of it."

Frank spoke, but his eyes remained shut.

"The first thing I saw when I arrived in the walled yard by the scullery was the dagger. I picked it up and only then saw Sir Sandoe slumped on the floor. At first, I thought he'd fainted."

I couldn't understand why he'd think that and figured it required more explanation. "Fainted? What made you believe that?"

"Passed out, I suppose. Sir Sandoe liked his drink." Frank still spoke with his eyes closed, beads of sweat forming on his forehead. "I don't know why, but I felt as if I were being observed. That's when I turned to the scullery window. Mrs Mullins, Dolly Trimmings, and you stared back. All hell broke loose, and I ran."

"But why pick up the dagger?"

"It looked familiar." Frank's eyes snapped open. He reached into his jacket pocket, retrieved his dagger, and held it up.

"Tony gave this to me on my last visit."

"Tony?"

"Miss Antoinette. I called her Tony." A sheen of perspiration covered his face.

I already knew about the romance so didn't press the issue. Instead, I sat still and waited.

"The plan was to run away to America." Frank was speaking slowly and trying to think the thing out while he talked. "But I wanted to earn some money first, so we'd have a cushion. I went to work in Africa, on the land, farming. Then after a fruitless year or two, I headed to India then back to England and my home town of Middleham in Yorkshire."

I stared hard at his glistening face. "But why a dagger?"

"Tony couldn't 'ave a ring as the servants would find it, and anyway I didn't 'ave money for that. Just enough for our passage to America, then I'd find a job." He paused and was silent for a few moments. "Tony gave me a dagger, and she kept one back for herself. A replica. 'Twas symbolic of us killing our old lives, I suppose."

I glanced at Uncle Tristan. He leaned forward on the stool, the orange glow of the lamp emphasising the whites in his eyes, which were open very wide.

"So," Frank said, speaking more slowly than ever now and so quietly, I had to hold my breath to hear him. "I saw the knife and picked it up. But it wasn't Tony's dagger."

"How do you know?"

His eyes closed for an instant, and then he gulped. "Because I etched a special message on the inside handle." He handed me the dagger and pointed. "Look close."

Under the flickering light, the letters XOT were faint but visible. I recalled Dr Swensen found a similar inscription on the dagger found in Miss Antoinette's chest.

I said, "What does the inscription mean?"

"Lots of kisses and hugs, and the T is for Tony. I inscribed the letters on two daggers: mine and Tony's."

I said, "Where did Miss Antoinette get the daggers?"

Frank smiled. "She swiped them from Lady Herriman's rooms. There were five in total, all identical. Real Victorian craftmanship and stored in an elegant wooden display case."

I shifted in my chair. His eyes followed me, and I could see he was wondering what I made of his story. Five daggers, with three accounted for. One in Frank's hand, one that killed Sir Sandoe, another found in the chest of Miss Antoinette. That left two. Where were they?

Frank continued, "Tony planned to return the knives as soon as she found it."

"Found what?"

Again, Frank smiled. "Tony liked languages and history. She was searching for Roman treasure."

"Albina's Hoard," said Uncle Tristan, with a gasp.

"Aye, that'd be it," said Frank. "Tony thought it was buried in the grounds of Bagington Hall. Anyway, the dagger that killed Sir Sandoe ain't my dagger."

I shifted again, trying to think of the best way forward. What was Frank doing outside the scullery window? Who killed Sir Sandoe? Was it the same person who murdered Miss Antoinette? And why? And there was the disappearance of Lady Sandoe. A thousand other questions bubbled in my mind. But I said, "How did you get into the scullery yard?"

"With my help," said Uncle Tristan. "Sir Sandoe left a note in the carriage house envelope rack with an instruction it be hand delivered to Frank. But Boots was too busy to go to the gatehouse. I'd seen Frank earlier, so I offered to deliver it for him."

I mulled this over for a moment then turned to Frank. "What did the note say?"

"Meet me by the scullery window in thirty minutes, but don't let anyone see you. And bring the envelope."

I said, "That's all?"

Frank nodded. "And with Mr Harbottle's help, I sneaked into the scullery yard."

I turned to Uncle Tristan. "How on earth did you get away with that?"

He looked at the ceiling, closed his eyes, and opened them again. "The note was a fake. Whoever wrote it set Frank up!"

"Okay," I said, standing and pacing the minuscule space, "so Frank didn't kill Sir Sandoe, but who did?"

Frank's eyes followed me as I moved. "Same person who did in"—his voice caught in his throat—"my Tony."

For about five seconds, there was silence. Then speaking slowly, I said, "Think back to when you discovered Sir Sandoe. Did you see who took the silver envelope from his body?"

"I've already asked him that," interrupted Uncle Tristan with a hint of annoyance.

Frank shook his head. "I scrambled over that wall and got away as quick as I could. 'Twas in his hand when I left." He turned to Uncle Tristan. "Thank you once again for slowing 'em down, else I'd be in a prison cell, and that's a fact."

"Shhh! For God's sake, man," whispered Uncle Tristan.

His concern was understandable. Aiding a murderer came with a lengthy prison sentence, or at worst, the hangman's noose. I changed the subject. "What was in the envelope?"

"Dunno, Tony mailed it to me sister's 'ouse in Middleham, Yorkshire, cos I was overseas and 'ad frequent changes of address. I came back from India two weeks ago."

I said, "That's when you first saw the silver envelope?"

"Aye, it came with a note from Tony that instructed me to give it to Sir Sandoe."

"Why?"

He shrugged. "Tony wrote if anything happened to her, he'd know what to do. Got involved with the agricultural union and came 'ere as quick as possible." His face slackened, eyes swollen and moist. "Tony's death is a terrible blow."

There wasn't much doubt in my mind about the truth of his story. But without the original letter, there was only his word, and that wouldn't go far if he was arrested for murder.

I said, "Are you sure you don't know what Miss Antoinette wrote in the letter?"

Frank walked with leaden feet back to his stool. "I know what she wrote. I made a copy." He reached into his jacket pocket, pulled out a crumpled slip of paper, and with eyes cast down, said, "But I don't know what it means."

Uncle said, "Good God, man, why didn't you say so! Here, let me see."

For several moments, we sat in silence as Uncle Tristan's eyes darted back and forth across the page. The oil lamp hissed and crackled. At last, he let out an exasperated sigh. "Looks like the scribblings of a madman. Maggie, come see."

I squinted in the dim light. Frank's penmanship was that of a drunken spider. But his faint scratching was legible, if unintelligible, to anyone who didn't read Gaelic. I spoke out loud as I translated.

"You shall find it in the West Wood, fifty paces from the river-bank, to the side of the overhanging ledge. A twisted oak lies to the left." I looked up. "What on earth does it mean?"

Frank said, "Sounds like the location of—"

"Dear God!" Uncle Tristan jumped to his feet, arms in the air. His eyes were bright now and wide open. "Gold! It's instructions to Albina's Hoard."

Uncle pranced in a tiny circle. "We're rich! Maggie, the treasure will more than cover our losses. Everything will be tickety-boo!"

Frank watched out of the sides of his eyes. "Won't do me no good on the gallows."

For the first time, Uncle raised his voice to almost a shout. "Now listen here! We'll be having none of that talk. There'll be more than enough to set you up for life in America. I have a contact in the town of Dover who'll secure your passage to Texas. Lie low for a few more weeks, and then I'll help you slip out of the country. Did it all the time in my circus days, and with gold in your pockets, you'll be set up for life."

Frank was on his feet now, the two men moving around each other like joyful Morris dancers.

I said, "But what about the murderer? We can't let them get away."

They sat down.

Frank said, "You are right, Miss Darling. I can't leave England until the police have caught Tony's killer."

Uncle Tristan stood up, walked over to Frank, and touched his shoulder. "Then we've got to give them a helping hand, and be quick about it."

"How?" asked Frank.

We fell into a glum silence. Chief Inspector Little was on the hunt for Frank Perry. There was no other person in his sights. Unless the killer turned themself in, there was little chance the murderer would be brought to justice.

Uncle rose to his feet and paced to the door. "Maggie, how many people read Gaelic?"

"Very few."

"Then the treasure is safe, for now. Come, I shall walk you home, and tomorrow we shall return to the woods of Bagington Hall to dig our own gold. Then we shall turn our attention to solving the murder of Sir Sandoe."

Chapter 56

LATER THAT NIGHT, I stood by the bedroom window watching Uncle Tristan skip away along the gravel path. I thought about Miss Antoinette. From what I'd learned, she was a resourceful young woman, independent and determined to carve her own future. The letter to Frank Perry was her insurance policy.

When Uncle disappeared through the garden gate, I gazed at the shadows dancing across the face of the moon. Suddenly overcome with fatigue, I drew the curtains, crawled into bed, and fell asleep, but my rest was fitful, punctuated by an indelible dream.

I sat on a bench under a tall oak tree looking across Saint Magdalene's graveyard. A bright sun warmed my face. I could see the meadow and hear the tinkle of water from the little stream. The sweet scent of mown grass filled my nostrils. I thought about how peaceful it was.

"Maggie!"

It was Mother's voice.

I looked around, but she was neither in front nor behind.

"Maggie!"

I looked up.

At the top of a long flight of stairs stood Mother. Not her face, but her back, hunched, leaning into the white light that emanated from a doorway.

"I'm coming," I called out, clambering to my feet. I took the stairs two at a time. "Almost there."

Feet moving faster than I could imagine, I made rapid progress. Two steps from the top, Mother turned around, her face in shadow.

"Be persistent but polite," she said then vanished.

Bewildered, I spun around. The bedsheets tumbled to the floor. I sat up. Gradually, consciousness crept in, sleep faded, but the vivid voice of Mother remained.

I walked to the bedroom window, pulled back the curtains, and peered through the glass. The sun was just coming up, partially hidden by a row of trees. Awake, but not yet alert, I lifted the metal latch and pushed.

The window swung open.

Oak, and sage, and the faint tint of fresh tobacco drifted in on the morning air. With deep breaths, I sucked it in then exhaled.

Wide awake, I glanced at the clock. Six a.m. Mrs Rusbridger wouldn't even be stirring. She served breakfast late on Sunday. Then at ten o'clock, I'd meet Uncle Tristan at the gate by the lane.

Feeling at a loose end, I sat at the writing desk and flipped open my journal. The solution to this puzzle lay with logic.

I thought about the killer. What did I know?

Nothing.

I tried asking a question.

"Why did Miss Antoinette ask Frank Perry to personally deliver a letter to the man who would oppose their marriage?"

Nothing.

But I wasn't ready to give up. I'd read that drawing random shapes triggers the logical brain into action. I picked up a pencil and doodled in my journal.

After ten minutes of random scribbles, I said, "It makes little sense."

I gave up on logic, closed my eyes, and let my unconscious mind take the lead.

The elongated face, weathered skin, and wide, dark eyes of Sir Sandoe stared back. He lay crumpled on the ground outside the scullery window. Even in death, his owl-like eyes seemed to take in everything all at once. And then there was the blood.

My eyes snapped open. The shock of his murder still rattled me. "No, wait!"

There was something about the man's face.

Again, I closed my eyes and concentrated.

Then I saw it. His expression. Was it fear?

"No, no, astonishment!"

My mouth formed an O as my eyes widened.

"Sir Sandoe knew his murderer!"

I lowered my eyelids in search of further inspiration. The minutes flashed by as I concentrated. Gradually, an image formed, blurred at first, then sharpening into a hairline moustache.

"Withers!"

With an eager hand, I printed his name in large letters at the top of a blank page. All I needed now was evidence to put the fiend behind bars.

"But who else would want Sir Sandoe dead?"

Lady Herriman did not hide her contempt. Dolly Trimmings had been duped by the prospect of gold. Boots suffered the indignity of a horsewhipping, and Mrs Mullins' complaints to Sir Sandoe about Withers' abuse of the staff fell on deaf ears.

And then there was the possibility the killer might be a visitor familiar with the grounds. But who? I thought of Tommy Crabapple with his crippled legs, of George Edwards the union organiser, and even of Vicar Humberstone with his bow and quiver filled with arrows. And then I thought of Frank Perry. I stopped there. Everyone had a motive.

I put the pencil down, closed the journal, and let out a miserable sigh.

Chapter 57

PARKING NEAR THE ENTRANCE of Bagington Hall with Frank Perry lying low in the back wasn't the best way to slip into the grounds unnoticed.

But Frank insisted on speaking with George Edwards, so we sat in the motorcar on the grassy verge, a little distance away from the main gates.

It was like a carnival. Tablecloths spread on long wooden benches; red, white, and blue bunting; flags; and lots and lots of protestors. Women, men, small children with their pets. They all congregated around the entrance where the gatekeeper stood, arms folded, flanked by Sergeant Pender and a handful of constables.

"Seems like the whole village," I muttered.

"And the Cromer Police Department," added Uncle Tristan, casting an anxious glance at Sergeant Pender.

Frank eased himself up to look through the window. "Would be nice to grab a bite to eat from one of those tables."

"Good God, man! Get down, or we'll all swing," cried Uncle Tristan.

Frank lowered himself down, grumbling as he did so.

"Do you think," I said in a slow voice, "we ought to postpone our treasure hunt until Monday? How can we search for Albina's Hoard with all of Cromer about us?"

Uncle Tristan rubbed his chin. "Everyone is here at the front gate. That leaves the West Wood wide open for us to explore. Now all we have to do is find George Edwards, let Frank have his chat, and everything will be tickety-boo."

I wasn't convinced and said, "Maybe we should come back tonight."

"Too dark," said Uncle Tristan. "We'd stumble around, and our oil lamps might draw the attention of the gamekeeper."

Uncle eased the motorcar door open. "Come on, Maggie, let's speak with George Edwards." He took off with long prancing steps, his Victorian cape flapping like the wings of a giant seabird.

I clambered onto the grassy verge. Uncle Tristan was already twenty yards ahead of me. I walked at a slow pace, afraid to move quicker in case I caught the attention of Sergeant Pender.

Vicar Humberstone stood on a soapbox with a large Bible in his right hand. At his side rested a bow with a quiver full of arrows. A small group of villagers gathered around as he delivered his Sunday sermon.

As I drew closer, I stopped to listen, and soon I spotted George Edwards. He leaned against the stone wall, watching. His hand dipped into a brown bag and flipped a cobnut into his mouth. He chewed as the vicar's sermon reached its crescendo. Then he spat the remnants back into the bag.

A hand tapped my shoulder. I turned around.

"Hullo, luv, thought it was you," said Hilda Ogbern. Dobbin was at her side, tail swishing back and forth.

"Hello, Hilda," I said. "Hello, Dobbin."

The dog rolled over. I rubbed his stomach.

Hilda said, "He's been tugging on the leash all morning. Suppose all these crowds excite him."

"Dobbin just needs a bit of attention," I said as I continued to rub his stomach.

"Aye, 'tis true enough."

I glanced towards Sergeant Pender. He was deep in conversation with the gatekeeper. A large group of men cycled in a circle in front of the gate. Uncle Tristan was alongside George Edwards and pointing in the direction of his motorcar.

"They say it will be a long strike," said Hilda. "Things ain't easy for Harold and me, but we'll stick it out a little while yet."

Dobbin tugged at the leash and broke free.

"Dobbin!"

But Dobbin didn't stop. The large hound didn't even look around as the leash dragged along the ground. He bounded away from the gates around a corner and disappeared.

"I'm not chasing after him," said Hilda. "He'll 'ave to find his own way back to our cottage."

"I think he'll be fine," I said, knowing the dog had a good nose for home.

"Aye, reckon your right." Hilda placed her hands on her hips. "More excitement 'ere than we've 'ad all year. What with Dobbin runnin' off, the strike, the vicar preaching brimstone and fire at the gates of the ole 'ouse, and now"—her voice filled with a tone of eager expectation—"you and Mr Harbottle is 'ere."

"Pardon?"

Hilda glanced around, shifting her weight from one foot to the other, looking as though she wanted to say something but needed a little prod.

I said, "What's the news?"

She turned towards the vicar and back then took a deep breath. "They say your uncle cast a spell to call upon Black Shuck to deliver another body before nightfall."

Dear God! Was there no end to the rumours? "Where on earth did you hear that?"

Hilda continued, "Since Lady Herriman is an old bird, me and Harold figured she'd be next."

"Utter nonsense."

But Hilda was enjoying herself too much to take any notice. "Don't likes to ask, but Mr Harbottle's cape got me thinkin'. Is it true he is one of those druids?"

"No," I snapped, "we are not druids, neither are we engaged in witchcraft or any other such occultist practices."

Hilda eyed me with disappointment. "That's what I told Boots when he got to jabbering about a curse."

"Utter nonsense," I repeated. "Not a shred of truth in it."

"I always said you is a God-fearing woman," replied Hilda. "And so is Mr Harbottle, in his own way. Anyone throw a curse on you, and it will only double back."

Again, I said, "There is no curse."

"What curse?" The question came from Mrs Mullins. She hurried over to join us.

"The one over Mr Harbottle's staffing agency," said Hilda, eager to keep the theme going.

"Oooh, so it's true, 'tis it?" Mrs Mullins' eyes shone with excitement.

I said, "Ladies, you ought to know better! And with the vicar delivering his sermon only a few feet away. There is no curse."

"Just repeating what I heard," said Hilda. "Thought I ought to let you know. Neighbourly thing to do, ain't it?"

Mrs Mullins said, "It ain't nothing to do with Miss Darling that we've had two bodies in less than a week, and we've never seen the likes of in Cromer before. No, no, she ain't cursed."

"Well, Mrs Mullins," I said with a hint of annoyance, "need I remind you that you were also at the scene of both bodies. So if there is a curse, it must be to do with you!"

"Ahhh," cried Hilda, "never thought of that. Mrs Mullins, what you been up to in that scullery of yours?"

"Don't be ridiculous." Mrs Mullins stamped her foot. "Stick to the facts."

"Well, 'ere is a fact and a good one," replied Hilda. "Norwich Bank 'ave hired a detective to investigate Sir Sandoe's financial affairs."

Hilda's face gleamed as she watched the astonished expressions on our faces.

I said, "From Scotland Yard?"

Hilda shook her head. "Nope."

"Then who?" asked Mrs Mullins.

"Chief Inspector Little. There'll be a write-up in the *Norfolk News*."

Mrs Mullins laughed. "The only thing that lazy sod will get to the bottom of is a tankard of apple cider."

There was a murmur of agreement.

Mrs Mullins said, "There ain't nothing but rumours and speculation in the newspaper these days. And such tittle-tattle don't count as facts in my book. "

Hilda said, "Well, 'ave you got anything better?"

"Oh yes," said Mrs Mullins. "Here is a real fact for you. Lady Herriman fired Dolly Trimmings, but—"

"Everyone knows that," said Hilda, cutting her off in mid-sentence. "I even knows she is living in the horse stable, and her last day is tomorrow. Next you'll be tellin' me Sir Sandoe is dead! What's the good sharing facts that everyone knows?"

Mrs Mullins snorted. "But do you know about Withers?"

"No," Hilda and I said simultaneously.

Mrs Mullins lowered her voice to a whisper. "The wedding is off. Her Ladyship fired him, and Dolly Trimmings 'as got her old job back."

Chapter 58

MY MOUTH OPENED IN astonishment at Mrs Mullins' news then snapped tight shut as my eyes bugged, and a slither of fear rippled along my spine.

Sergeant Pender strode towards us, his eyes fixed and earnest. Constable Lutz hurried at his side.

"Mornin', Officers," said Hilda as they drew near. "Nice day for it."

I froze, my mouth open, throat bone dry.

"Good day, ladies," mumbled the sergeant, his eyes fixed on some point in the distance.

We followed his gaze to Uncle Tristan's motorcar. George Edwards leaned against the door. Inside, I could make out the head of Frank Perry. He peeped through the open window, and his lips moved fast as if conveying a lot of information.

The officers continued their march.

A cry came from the entrance to Bagington Hall. The thud of feet landing on the grass combined with shouts.

"Stop! Wait!"

Uncle Tristan ran after the police officers with galloping strides, cape flapping, arms waving. I charged after him.

Sergeant Pender swung around, raised a hand in a salute, and turned back, picking up his pace.

Frank ducked down.

George Edwards lifted his eyes, turned, and with surprising fleetness for one so old, took off towards the stone wall.

Like a greyhound after a hare, the officers changed direction, scurrying after the old man.

George Edwards scrambled up the wall, balanced on the top, and raised his arms high in the air like an excited politician.

"We'll not end this strike until we gets fair pay for fair wages," he yelled.

Sergeant Pender and Constable Lutz stood in silence, contemplating whether to go after the union organiser. They waited too long. A crowd gathered—strikers—men and women with faces that showed they worked hard to earn less than they needed.

A murmur of excitement flowed through the throng. They were eager to hear the encouraging words of the union organiser.

"We'll not give in to them in London or be forced into surrender by the local police."

A wild cheer went up from the crowd.

"Come on," I said, catching up to Uncle Tristan and grabbing his arm. "Let's leave before Sergeant Pender remembers he wanted to investigate the contents of your motorcar. And thank God George Edwards' decoy trick worked!"

Chapter 59

I WAS WET, COLD, AND tired, but although we'd followed the instructions of Miss Antoinette's letter, there was no sign of Albina's Hoard.

Uncle Tristan tugged at a root with his bare hands, slipped, and cursed as he fell onto the stony soil at one end of a shallow trench. His mud-splattered face looked at me. "Are you sure this is the right spot?"

For the tenth time, I pointed to the overhanging ledge and the ancient, twisted oak. "About fifty paces from the river. This is it."

"Aye," added Frank on his knees, digging with a shovel, his sweat-soaked shirtsleeves rolled up. "Albina's Hoard 'tis buried in this pit somewhere."

"Maggie, reread the letter to me," said Uncle Tristan, arms rested on the shovel.

"No, keep digging." The shadows were already lengthening. Dusk would bring an end to our treasure hunt. "Else we must come back tomorrow."

Uncle Tristan brought down the shovel with a resounding thud. Pebbles and earth flew in the air, revealing only more of the same underneath.

"Arrgh!" He threw the shovel on the ground. "I'm tired of breathing in dirt. Where's the treasure?"

"Come on, Uncle, I reckon we're less than three feet from gold." But I wondered if we were on a wild-goose chase. Did Miss Antoinette have a warped sense of humour? Was the letter a youthful prank?

A snort mingled with the sharp clang of the shovels.

"Shhh! What's that?" asked Uncle Tristan.

We listened.

The noise came again. An occasional snort from beyond a clump of bushes on the bank that sloped up to our left. I moved closer to the sound while the men watched. It was then I saw him: Dobbin, paws high up a tree trunk, sniffing and snorting.

"It's Hilda Ogbern's new puppy," I said, moving up the slope.

"He's a big 'un for a pup," said Frank.

"Keep digging while I catch him, and we can take him back to Cromer with us."

"If there is room in the motorcar," said Uncle Tristan. "Albina's Hoard might take up all the space."

"There'll be space," I said. "If not, you must make two trips."

I left the men to their digging and climbed the shallow incline towards the bushes and Hilda's dog.

"Dobbin, come here."

But Dobbin, with a taste for freedom, dropped from the tree trunk and squirmed through a gap in the shrubs.

Gasping with annoyance and clinging to low tree branches for support, I tried to follow the lively hound. A branch snagged my coat.

"Dobbin, come here!" I shrieked.

Drawing in a deep breath, I untangled myself from the branch and eased through a narrow gap, sidestepping sharp thorns.

There were trees and bushes in every direction but not a sign of Hilda Ogbern's dog.

"Oh bother!"

Retracing my steps, I began the downward walk back to Frank and Uncle Tristan. And then it happened. If only I'd have been nearer, I would have seen the whole incident unfold.

"Found it!" Uncle Tristan's voice carried through the trees.

"God bless Tony," cried Frank.

"Wrapped in cloth," said Uncle Tristan, his voice filled with excitement. "Help me tug the thing."

The voices went quiet.

For almost a minute, the woods became still. No bird chirps, no breeze, not even the hum of insects.

A fierce cry broke the calm.

It rang out above the trees followed by a sharp thwack. The dull thud repeated four or five times.

I scrambled down the incline. At the edge of the bushes where the ground levelled, I stopped. Steadying myself on a tree trunk, I gazed towards the area where the men had been digging.

Uncle Tristan lay sprawled on the ground, his arms askew. Next to him, Frank Perry rolled around on the edge of the shallow pit bawling in pain.

Chapter 60

WHAT ON EARTH?

I crouched low, watching.

"Me leg's broken. For God's sake, man. Me leg is broken." Frank clutched his right leg.

A figure stood over him.

With a start, I realised it was Withers. He held a horsewhip in his right hand.

I crouched even lower.

"Man, 'ave a little mercy," said Frank.

Withers raised his arm high in the air. The horsewhip came down with his full body weight. Frank let out a low groan, twitched, and became still.

"Dear God!" I whispered.

For a split second, I considered rushing from my hiding place to confront the evil man but immediately dismissed the thought. He'd already knocked down two men. I'd suffer the same fate. How could I even the odds?

My mind worked fast. Soon I had a plan. It was simple. When Withers turned his back, distracted by the find, I'd rush forward, grab the shovel or horsewhip, and let him have it. I licked my lips at the thought, and as tight as a coil, I watched and waited for my chance.

Withers stared at the unmoving figures, his body jerking in deep, gasping breaths. At last, he let the horsewhip fall to the ground and stripped off his jacket. A silver envelope peeped out of the side pocket.

I let my breath out slowly. The odds were tipping in my favour. On a count of three, I told myself, as he climbed into the shallow trench.

"One."

With a grunt, he dropped to his knees. Only his head was visible. The sound of his hand clawing at the soil echoed through the still air. "The old witch can throw me out of Bagington Hall, but this treasure is mine."

"Two."

The scraping stopped. Withers grunted like an impatient pig at mealtime. "I have it!"

"Three."

He was laughing now.

I lurched forward, hurling myself down the slope, fury blazing in my eyes.

What happened next occurred with such speed, I'm not sure I took it all in.

"What the..." Withers scrambled from the trench. His shoulders trembled. The shudder moved like a wave along his back. When it reached his legs, they collapsed, throwing him face first back into the pit.

Just as he clambered out a second time, Dolly Trimmings appeared. She charged towards the man, a long-handled dagger in her right hand.

At the last moment, Withers saw the threat. In a quick movement, he reached for his horsewhip. But she was upon him before he took aim.

"You lied to me about the gold mines," she squealed.

"Only way to get an ounce of work from your lazy butt."

They struggled, twisting and turning, making it hard to see exactly what was happening. Dolly let out a savage growl; Withers slipped; the dagger plunged down, striking him in the chest. He let out a thin, high-pitched wail. It sounded close yet far away. A wretched, soulless whine.

Again, Dolly struck, and again. And now she was laughing.

Withers' feet went out from under him casting him forward back into the pit.

Momentum carried me to the edge of the trench. At the bottom, underneath Withers and wrapped in a ragged, torn sheet, part of a blackened leg stuck out. I felt my stomach churn, stumbled, corrected myself, but twisted my left knee: the strength oozed from it.

I heard laughter behind me and turned to see Dolly, the bloodied dagger in her steady hand.

"Sorry, Miss Darling," she said quietly, her birdlike eyes twitching. "You have found my secret."

I let out a ragged breath, trying to ignore the shooting pain from my knee. There was no chance of running. I played for time. "Why did you kill Miss Antoinette?"

"She was poking around the grounds for treasure but figured out what I done with her mother. Told me all about it, she did. So I had to do her in." Dolly's broad lips tugged into a grin. "Miss Antoinette was as nosy as 'er mother." Dolly nodded towards the pit, leaving no doubt about the identity of the corpse.

"But why did you kill Lady Sandoe?"

"The woman strongly objected to my entrepreneurial activities."

"You mean stealing from Bagington Hall?"

"Gave me a week to turn myself in, she did. But that would've meant time in a cold, hard prison cell. And I likes me plum wine and me pearls and me fine gowns."

"Put the dagger down," I said. "Let's talk about this before any more damage is done."

"No, no, Miss Darling," she snarled. "Got me job back with Her Ladyship, I 'ave. You'll 'ave to die here. Then I can thinks about me plan." She nodded towards Frank. "He'll swing for the lot of yer. Including Withers who got what he deserved."

She stepped forward, dagger ready to strike.

I placed weight on my left leg and clenched my teeth with the pain. "Tell me how you knew we'd be here."

"I didn't," she growled. "But guessed. Old Dolly forgot the envelope when I killed Sir Sandoe. I knew it was from Miss Antoinette. But I only remembered the darn thing when I looked through the scullery window. Then it was gone. Me thinks it must 'ave been Withers or Mr Harbottle or Boots. I didn't know who, so I waited to see who'd show up."

I could wait no longer. I hurled myself at Dolly. She lurched forward with the dagger. It sliced through the sleeve of my right arm. Again, she jabbed, this time drawing blood.

I had a flash of realisation that Dolly Trimmings was about to end my life, here in the shallow grave of Lady Sandoe, where the truth might never be uncovered. I thought of Father and Nancy as an angry growl roared in my ears, somehow louder, more savage than before.

Dolly stumbled forward. I sidestepped and gasped at the sight of Dobbin with his fat paws clawing at her back. She toppled into the pit, followed by the puppy who pinned her with his weight, his chest rumbling with a low growl.

"Goodness, I only wanted a partridge for my supper." Vicar Humberstone emerged from the bushes, bow in hand. "Miss Darling, I was about to unleash an arrow or two, but Dobbin saved me the trouble."

Chapter 61

TEN DAYS LATER

"I've always kept away from them." Uncle Tristan shuddered. He sat at his writing desk in the loft office. "What with all that white powder, orange hair, and oversized shoes. When I was Lord Avalon, Man of Mystery, I kept well clear. Clowns can't be trusted."

"Who'd 'ave thought they'd have so much strength?" Frank rubbed his bruised face. "Light footed and sneaky too. Didn't even see Withers coming till he was on me with that horsewhip."

"Ah, surprise!" Uncle Tristan jumped to his feet. "That's what I'm telling you. It is what clowns do, jump out at people to startle them. There is no place for that in a circus. Mystery and magic, yes—shock, no!"

"Dolly Trimmings surprised all of us, including Withers," I said. "But she was even more surprised when Sergeant Pender and Constable Lutz carted her off. I've never heard such a stream of foul language, not even in the pie-and-mash shop."

We fell into a moment of contemplation.

"Vicar Humberstone did a respectable job with Withers' funeral," said Uncle Tristan. "It surprised me to see so many people turn out."

"The whole village," muttered Frank. "Probably makin' sure the bugger was dead."

"Frank Perry!" I said, "Show some respect. Withers was a repugnant character, but that didn't make his cold-blooded murder right."

Uncle Tristan changed the subject. "The vicar did a wonderful job with Lady Sandoe. I didn't know the woman but shed a tear or two."

Landowners from Cromer and the surrounding villages attended the service. Household staff from the Blackwood, Matthews, and Bagington estates formed a line of honour as the pallbearers carried the coffin. I felt a deep pang of sadness watching Lord and Lady Blackwood stand side by side with a weeping and dishevelled Lady Herriman.

"Aye." Frank's voice caught. "I'm comforted in the knowledge me Tony is with her mother."

Uncle stood, placed an arm across Frank's shoulder, and said, "Won't be long before Dolly Trimmings is in court. Can't see a judge letting her off now she's confessed. One count of murder is bad enough, but four!"

"At least we know what happened to the missing daggers," I said. "Dolly had one, and the other was with Lady Sandoe's body."

"Aye, and I gets to keep the one Tony gave me. Didn't see the point of mentioning it to Chief Inspector Little." Frank's lips curved into a sad smile. "Half of me wants to stay for the sentencing, but I'm not one to relish in the troubles of others."

I said, "That's why you are leaving?"

Frank nodded. "From Southampton in the morning. Chief Inspector Little said it would be fine on account they 'ave enough evidence for her to swing, but that don't bring me no pleasure. I won't forget me Tony, but I'm goin' to make a new life in America. That's want she would 'ave wanted."

Chapter 62

A SHARP KNOCK ON THE office door interrupted our conversation.

"Come in," shouted Uncle Tristan.

The door swung open, and Boots hurried into the room. His shoes shone like polished glass, suit crisp and new, and the collars to his bright white shirt were as stiff as planks of wood.

His long neck drooped, and he made a low bow.

"'Ave a guest for yer."

"Oh, don't be so formal," said Mrs Mullins, following him into the room. Rose held her arm. "I'm Her Ladyship's new chambermaid, not bloody royalty."

Uncle and Frank clambered to their feet.

"Sit down," said Mrs Mullins. "Like I says, I ain't royalty. But I sure like me new workin' conditions. I'm even getting a taste for plum wine, but that's where it stops." She eased herself onto a seat. "Rose, you sit next to Miss Darling."

Uncle Tristan and Frank sat.

When Mrs Mullins settled into the seat, she said, "Now I guess you is wondering what I'm doing 'ere?"

"Indeed I am," said Uncle Tristan with a hint of caution in his voice. "I'm afraid if Lady Herriman is suing for trespass, our pockets are empty."

"She ain't as hard hearted as Sir Sandoe and—"

"Tell her about the news," interrupted Boots, his narrow eyes opened wide. "Else it'll be all over Cromer before you get to say a word."

Mrs Mullins breathed in as if savouring the pungent odour. "Loves the scent of curing hides. Me father used to work the chemicals on our little farm." Again, she breathed in. "Lady Herriman's nephew from Scotland is coming down to help 'ere run the estate. He'll be here next week. That's why I'm 'ere."

"Very good," said Uncle. "But what has that to do with us?"

"Her Ladyship's changed since Withers has gone. That pendant of his had some devious power over her. I reckon when she gave him his marching orders, it broke the spell. I wouldn't say she has a heart of gold. But she donated to Saint Magdalene's and told the vicar he could hunt in West Wood whenever he wants."

I wondered whether the hunt would be as much fun for the vicar. Part of his joy lay in the illicit nature of his archery activities.

Mrs Mullins searched into a handbag and pulled out a docket filled with papers. "Lady Herriman has changed her mind on account of your help in solving the mystery of Bagington Hall. She would like to hire Tristan's Hands."

Uncle jumped to his feet, pranced in front of his desk, and took Mrs Mullins by the shoulders, planting a kiss on her cheek.

"Fancy that," she said, her lips breaking out into a broad smile. Again, she reached into her handbag and pulled out a slip of paper and handed it to Uncle Tristan.

He stared at it for a moment, then his body became very stiff. "Surely there is a mistake?"

"Lady Herriman said this belongs to you."

Uncle Tristan's face paled; his eyes became wide. "Maggie, it's your father's and my initial investment plus ten per cent."

Mrs Mullins grinned. "And Lady Herriman has asked if you would sign up Tommy Crabapple on your books."

"Pardon?"

"Her nephew will need a clerk, and I recommended him to the position. Even told her about the accident, I did, and she said she'd sort somethin' out for the boy."

Once again, Mrs Mullins searched in her bag. "Ah, here is a list of the vacant positions."

Uncle Tristan took the sheet of paper, placed it on his desk, pranced to my writing table, and took me by the hand. Together, we danced around the tiny loft above John and Sons butchers, shouting with joy and laughter.

Author's Note

NOTHING MAKES ME HAPPIER than the thought of a reader finishing one of my books.

So, thank you!

If you enjoyed this story, I hope you'll leave a review at the retail website where you bought it. Reviews help readers like you discover books they will enjoy and help indie authors like me improve our stories.

Until next time,

N.C. Lewis

P.S. As an indie author, I work hard to bring you entertaining cozy mysteries as fast as I can. I've got many more books in the works, and I hope you'll come along for the ride.

Be the First to Know

Want more stories like this? Sign up for my Mystery Newsletter[1] and be the first to know about new book releases, discounts and free books. Or visit: https://www.nclewis.com/newsletter.html

---

1. https://www.subscribepage.com/b8b7j4

Printed in Great Britain
by Amazon